DEATH OF AN ART COLLECTOR

ALSO BY ROBERT GOLDSBOROUGH

DEATH OF AN ART COLLECTOR

A Nero Wolfe Mystery

Robert Goldsborough

MYSTERIOUSPRESS.COM

OPEN ROAD
INTEGRATED MEDIA
NEW YORK

Copyright © 2019 by Robert Goldsborough

Cover design by Ian Koviak

Author photo by Colleen Berg

978-1-5040-5754-7

Published in 2019 MysteriousPress.com/Open Road Integrated Media, Inc.
180 Maiden Lane
New York, NY 10038
www.mysteriouspress.com
www.openroadmedia.com

To my grandsons, Rex Robert and

Robert Jameson, and to my

granddaughter Abigail Bridget

DEATH OF AN ART COLLECTOR

CHAPTER 1

Over the years, I have attended cocktail parties, dinners, dances, and myriad charitable events with Lily Rowan, some of them held in her duplex penthouse apartment on East Sixty-Third Street between Madison and Park Avenues. A few words about Lily: She is beautiful, rich, and—to use her own word—*lazy*. I take issue with the lazy part, however, because she has invariably used her inherited wealth to support good works, from orphanages and soup kitchens to shelters for the homeless and for unwed mothers.

I met Lily in a pasture in Upstate New York eons ago when a bull named Caesar charged at me, and to escape from his horns and his hooves I dove over a fence and sprawled at the feet of a lovely blonde wearing a yellow shirt and slacks, who clapped and said, "Beautiful, Escamillo! Do it again!"*

---

* From *Some Buried Caesar* by Rex Stout

I later learned that Escamillo is a toreador in the opera *Carmen*, and Lily has called me that ever since. She and I have a relationship that is nobody's business but ours. Her wealth comes from her late father, an immigrant from Ireland who made millions by building much of the New York City sewer system.

Just so that you understand, whenever Lily and I go out, whether to a dinner, dancing at the Churchill, a Broadway play, the opera, or a hockey game at Madison Square Garden, I pay.

On this balmy spring night in Manhattan, the kind the chamber of commerce extols, I accompanied Lily to a dinner in the ballroom at the Waldorf Astoria. This fest was held to give patrons of the new Guggenheim Museum—Lily being among them—a sneak preview of sorts, with photographs and architectural drawings, showing what to expect from this highly publicized and unconventional addition to New York's museum scene, which was still in its construction stages.

We were seated at a table with six other people whom I had never seen with one exception. Lily seemed to have met them all, hardly a surprise given her crowded social calendar and wide circle of acquaintances. On my right was the most attractive woman in the group, other than Lily, of course. She introduced herself as Nadia Wordell, a slender redhead who I guessed to be in her mid to late twenties. Her dimpled smile more than made up for a nose that was a shade too small, and I liked her modest demeanor, which made her even more appealing.

Next to Nadia sat her father, Arthur Wordell, short and thin to the point of being gaunt, who possessed an impressive mane of white hair and looked as if he should be her grandfather, since he appeared to be about seventy-five. I soon learned through the chatter around me that he was expected to donate some or all of his large and highly valued collection of art to the new museum.

Wordell struck me from the first as a stuffed shirt. He acted as if he would rather be someplace else, although when any of the others at the table asked about his art, he puffed out his chest and fixed ice-blue eyes on his questioner.

"I know great art when I see it," he said, running a hand through that white hair. "I come by this instinctively. Not to share with the public in some way what I have amassed would be a sin—yes, indeed, a sin."

A narrow-faced, long-nosed woman named Faith Richmond, a biographer of nineteenth- and twentieth-century artists, peered through tortoiseshell glasses that grotesquely magnified her eyes. She told Wordell, "This is a wonderful thing you are doing, Arthur. Just wonderful. Your impressionist and postimpressionist works in particular will be an incredible asset to the Guggenheim if you choose to favor the new museum with your collection."

He threw a curt nod in her direction as a tuxedoed man whose center-parted black hair looked like it had been buffed with shoe polish stepped to the lectern, cleared his throat, and paused, letting the chatter die down. "Thank you all so very much for coming here this evening," he said in a radio-announcer voice that oozed sincerity. "I need not tell you these are exciting times indeed as we eagerly await the completion of the Solomon R. Guggenheim Museum, an institution to which all of you here have shown your unwavering loyalty.

"We had been hoping tonight to have the legendary architect Frank Lloyd Wright with us, but, unfortunately, Mr. Wright is unable to be in attendance because of a prior engagement.

"But despite the lack of his presence, we will have on the screen behind me depictions of the architect's genius, exterior examples that many of you have already seen as you have passed the intersection of East Eighty-Ninth Street and Fifth Avenue."

With that, our host put a black-and-white photograph of the museum's exterior on the giant screen to the accompaniment of "oohs" and "aahs." I had passed the structure myself on several occasions, and while I am by no means an expert on architectural styles or on the highly praised Mr. Wright, I found the building to resemble nothing more than a round layer-cake that was larger at the top than at the bottom. But then, what do I know about genius, other than that of the man who signs my checks? And even with my boss, Nero Wolfe, I make no claim to be able to keep up with his thought processes, which invariably leave me trailing in his wake.

Our speaker continued to show photographic slides of the unfinished interior of the museum and also some of the architect's conceptions of how the display areas would appear.

"One incredible feature of the Guggenheim," the emcee intoned, "is this ramp gallery that spirals downward from the top of the building. It is Mr. Wright's brilliant idea that visitors can ride an elevator up and then walk down the ramp, leisurely observing the wonderful art arrayed before them.

"That art originates, of course, from the glorious collection assembled by the late Mr. Guggenheim and will be added to by many other generous donors, including one who I am happy to report is present with us tonight . . . Arthur Wordell. Mr. Wordell, please stand and take a justly earned bow!"

But the man of the moment was by no means happy. He remained seated, scowled, and raised one arm briefly to the applause. After the clapping subsided, he muttered, to no one in particular, "I certainly did not expect or need that," and set his face in a frown that deepened his facial wrinkles.

"But, Arthur, the people were just showing their appreciation," said the lean and well-dressed Emory Sterling. I had learned through Lily and the table conversation that he was publisher of the New York–based magazine *Art & Artists.* "Those here tonight have a great admiration for you," Sterling went on. "Surely you cannot deny them the pleasure of giving you a form of thanks."

"I most certainly can deny them," Wordell shot back, stiffening, "especially as I have not yet committed to giving my works to this museum. I should get up and walk out of here right now, dammit!"

"Daddy—please, stay, please," Nadia said, putting a hand on his arm. "No one meant any harm."

He snorted and folded his arms across his chest and pouted like a petulant child. "I simply cannot believe the presumption of these people," he said. "If this is a feeble attempt to stampede me into making a decision, I can assure everyone that it will not succeed."

"Arthur, I agree with Emory and your lovely daughter," said Henry Banks, who I learned was the curator of several large private collections, and who, like Faith Richmond and Emory Sterling, was a member of an advisory board Wordell had cobbled together, presumably to help him decide about the future of his collection.

"I do not believe that anyone is trying to stampede you into anything, Arthur," Banks went on in a soothing tone. "If I were you, I would simply chalk it up to the naive exuberance of tonight's master of ceremonies. He of course has heard and read about the possibility of your bequeathing the collection to the Guggenheim—heaven knows that there has been enough speculation about it in print and around town in general. And he just made the irrational jump from rumor to reality. I would not take his words too seriously."

Wordell glowered at Banks but said nothing. The atmosphere at the table had become strained, but another of our number, the tweedy Boyd Tatum, a professor of fine arts at New York University, tried to lighten the mood by telling Wordell that, "You have truly become a man of mystery, Arthur, and after all, the world of the arts likes nothing more than a good mystery, which is why I want to write your story. The cognoscenti surely have been asking one another: Will he give his collection to the Guggenheim? Or perhaps to some another American museum? Or maybe to the Louvre or the Hermitage or to one of London's grand galleries? I suspect that you like to keep people guessing. Am I right about that?"

"Well . . . I like to take my time when making major decisions," Wordell muttered, glaring at Tatum and clearing his throat. "I have never been one to rush into anything. Just ask my daughter," he said, gesturing toward Nadia.

"He is absolutely right," she replied with a smile. "He once took months to decide to buy a Manet that had been offered to him. I thought the poor man who owned the oil was going to die of frustration before Daddy finally made up his mind."

That brought a good laugh from our tablemates, although Wordell refused to enter into the jollity. However, I could detect a slight sense of relief permeating the assemblage. The only other person at the table who rivaled Wordell in grumpiness was Roger Mason, a hollow-cheeked specimen whose thinning and once-black hair was tinged with white and who, Lily had informed me, was the curator of the Wordell collection.

Mason had sat expressionless and without speaking a word the entire evening. Lily also had told me that he was unhappy because Wordell had appointed that advisory group she had told me about, the one consisting of Banks, Sterling, and Faith Richmond. "My sources tell me that he is mad as hell and feels that he has been undercut by Wordell."

"You always seem to have very good sources," I told her. "Mark me down as impressed."

As our conversation continued in subdued tones, the master of ceremonies went on gushing and showing photos and architectural renderings of other features in the new museum.

"The art world has never seen anything like this and likely never will again," he said in somber tones as if narrating a newsreel. "Now it is not my purpose tonight to directly ask for contributions from you fine folks for this one-of-a-kind structure—I am confident most of you already have given generously—but I hope everyone here will continue to support the Guggenheim Museum with your time, your talent, and your treasures. It is indeed a worthy enterprise."

"The man has a way with words, doesn't he?" Lily whispered to me.

"Yeah, 'Charm us, Orator, till the Lion look no larger than the Cat.' "

"That's very good, Escamillo!" she said, clapping her hands. "Did you make that one up yourself?"

"Hardly," I laughed. "It's from a Tennyson poem titled 'Locksley Hall Sixty Years After.' And lest you accuse me of being highfalutin, I picked up the line from Wolfe. He used it when a pompous guy was spouting off in his office, and as you know, once I hear something, I never forget it."

"Maybe that is part of why I find you so fascinating."

"I can only hope."

"Well, I for one agree with Mr. Wordell that our master of ceremonies was shockingly presumptuous." That sentence came from the most unusual-looking individual in our group, an artist with the unlikely—and surely fabricated—name of Zondra Zagreb. She was the one individual in this artistic gathering I had met previously. Some months back, Lily had hauled me along to a showing of Miss Zagreb's work at a gallery up on Madison Avenue near the Metropolitan Museum. At the time, she had told me that "Zondra is one of America's great abstract expressionists, far more talented than Jackson Pollock could ever dream of being." Whoever he was.

Lily might be well right, but all I could make out at the time was what looked like someone had splattered paints of all colors on the canvases in no apparent pattern. I politely nodded and stroked my chin while gazing at these works, but I kept my opinions to myself lest I show my ignorance and I sipped the very good white wine being served by perky young women who weaved through the gallery wearing tuxedos, red bow ties, and smiles.

Now on to Miss Z's appearance this night at the Waldorf: Her crew cut had been dyed a shade of what I would term lilac, and she wore a muumuu that had at least as many colors as her artwork. She was clad in high-heeled gold sandals that showed off her toenails, each one painted in a different hue of the rainbow. She actually wasn't a bad-looking fortyish woman if you ignored the hair and the small gold ring in her nose, but she did stand out in this crowd like a belly dancer at an actuarial convention. Surely, shock was her intent.

"Come on, Arthur, honestly now, don'tcha think my work belongs in the new Guggie?" Zondra asked Wordell with a twinkle in her heavily made-up eyes. Despite her exotic name, she had no perceptible accent I could identify. The art collector frowned but then couldn't help himself and broke into a smile. "Why . . . yes, yes, Zondra, I guess it does," he replied, coloring slightly and actually chuckling. Her sassiness clearly worked on him, which was amusing to see.

"But of course, your work should hang in the new building, Zondra, there is no question about it," Faith Richmond put in. "If anyone were to ask my opinion, I would reply with a rousing yes!"

"Thank you, Faith," the crew-cut artist replied with a smirk. "I do so need more friends like you."

"We all are your friends here," Tatum told the flamboyant artist. "After all, you have justly received many fine reviews. I heartily agree with Faith that there must by all means be a place for your work in this Guggenheim edifice of Mr. Wright's."

"From your lips to God's ears, Boyd," she said with a toothy smile. "Maybe we should start a petition." That suggestion, whether or not serious, was met with raised brows, shrugs, and eye rolls. "You may not appreciate her art, Escamillo," Lily whispered to me, "but you have got to give the woman her due as a self-promoter."

"I will concede the point without an argument," I whispered back as our master of ceremonies droned on about the greatness of the new museum. His act was wearing thin, however, and the crowd showed signs of restlessness. Finally, sensing he might well be losing his audience, he showed one more photograph of the museum's exterior and thanked everyone for coming. I wasn't sure if the applause that followed was in appreciation for the program or in thanks because it was over.

"This is a watershed moment for both the arts community and for our great city as a whole," our emcee said. "I for one am proud to be witness to such a moment in New York's artistic history. I look forward to seeing all of you at the grand opening of the Guggenheim Museum." He closed with outstretched arms as if conferring a blessing upon the assemblage. The only word missing was an *amen!*

"Let us get ourselves out of here and into one of the watering holes in this fine hostelry for a nightcap," I told Lily, ever the social butterfly, who was busy saying her good-byes to our tablemates as they rose to leave. I was all but ignored, except by Zondra Zagreb, who took my hand in hers and, looking me square in the eye, said, "I am so happy to have seen you again, Mr. Goodwin. May I call you Archie?"

I told her she could and she said, "Please call me Zondra, and remember, that is with a 'Z.' I recall when you came to my showing at that gallery with Lily, who speaks so highly of you— and with good reason. I do so hope that we shall meet again."

I told her I hoped for the same thing and then left the ballroom with a smug-looking Lily on my arm. As we walked down a corridor toward the lobby, she leaned over and whispered in my ear, "Women just can't stay away from you, can they?"

"What can I say? I just try to be friendly to everyone."

CHAPTER 2

We settled into a booth in a dimly lit bar that occupied an alcove just off the lobby of the Waldorf and gave the waiter our order, scotch and water for each of us. "Well, what was your impression after having rubbed shoulders with some of the leading and not-so-leading lights of the local arts world?" Lily asked me with a wry grin.

"A singular group, without question," I replied. "Not a bunch I would choose to dine with, except maybe—"

"Maybe the fetching young Nadia Wordell?"

"To her credit, she seemed fairly normal, unlike—"

"Zondra Zagreb," Lily interrupted again.

"She definitely is in a class by herself, but then, as you remember, I have met her before."

"You have indeed, and it is crystal clear that the woman remains impressed with you. The next time I saw Zondra after we attended that showing of hers last year, she couldn't stop talking about how charming you were."

"It just shows that she has good taste."

"But you clearly don't think the same about her creations or her toenails," Lily said. "I saw you give them the once-over with raised eyebrows."

"Well, you have to remember that I am not qualified to discuss the quality of a given work of art or anything to do with women's fashions or cosmetics, so what I believe really doesn't count for anything."

"You are being far too modest. And whatever you may think about Zondra's talent, or her garb for that matter, I can tell you that behind that eccentric facade of hers is a very decent, talented individual whose real name happens to be Angela Baxter, originally of Altoona, Pennsylvania. But that is not for publication."

"Understood. Arthur Wordell is certainly one very dour specimen," I said, shifting gears.

"I can't say that I know him very well, Archie, but I agree that he hardly qualifies as 'Mr. Sunshine.' I have only met him at all because of his daughter, Nadia. She and I have served on a couple of boards together."

"So Miss Wordell, like you, gets involved in good works?"

"Nadia is a fine young woman, Wordell's only child, and a somewhat late-in-life arrival. And she puts up with her father's moods and eccentricities, which I have been told are numerous."

"Is Daddy Wordell married?"

"He has been legally separated for several years now. You may recall reading that he and Alexis Evans Farrell Wordell—and yes, she always uses all four names—got into a messy fight over money. She made a lot of demands, most of which he acceded to, but she kept upping the ante and asking for more."

"The man would seem to have plenty to give, though."

"No question whatever. His wealth is sizable and inherited; his New England father made his money, tons of it, in the

14

shipbuilding industry. It was once said that at least one out of every three merchant vessels sailing on the Atlantic at any given time was built by Elias Wordell."

"I gather Arthur has had to keep upping the ante to keep Alexis happy."

"To a point, and with increasing reluctance. But where he drew the line is when she began suggesting—and none too subtly at that—that she was entitled to a portion of his art collection upon his passing."

"That really had to frost the old boy."

Lily laughed. "That is putting it mildly. I don't closely follow the adventures of the Family Wordell, but the last I heard, Alexis was still trying to pry a good-sized portion of Arthur's collection out of him, and he was fighting like crazy to keep her from getting so much as a single canvas."

"Who do you think will win that battle?"

"I have only met Alexis on one occasion, and based on that brief encounter, I found her to be a tough cookie. Having said that, however, I think this is one battle that she's likely to lose."

"You mentioned earlier that Wordell is eccentric. In what ways does that manifest itself?"

"Most of what I know about him I've learned from his daughter," Lily said. "For instance, even though he is as rich as Croesus, he chooses to live relatively simply, given his wealth. Nadia says he owns a town house in the East Eighties that sounds like it's no bigger than the one where you and Nero Wolfe reside, and only a few pieces of his priceless art are on display there. She tells me that the rest is in storage."

"So the man is wealthy but definitely weird."

"There is more, Archie. He maintains an office, if you can term it that, in a nondescript Midtown building. According to Nadia, he has two rooms, sparsely furnished, about twenty floors up in an aging and not very well-maintained building just north of Times Square and slightly east of the Theater District. She says her father likes it because he's got some good views down on what he calls 'busy, hectic New York, with all of its sounds and smells and crowds.' "

"Does he have some sort of staff there?"

"If you want to call it that. One elderly woman who takes dictation and answers his phones—when she's there. And before you ask, I have no idea what Wordell accomplishes in this so-called place of business."

"With his dough, he doesn't have to accomplish a blasted thing, my dear. Ah, for the life of an eccentric. Remember, I do work for one."

"Yes, but Nero Wolfe acts positively proper compared to Mr. Wordell."

"I am not even sure why I'm bothering to ask about the man," I said.

"I was wondering that myself, Escamillo."

"For a reason I'm not able to put into words, I find myself wanting to know more about those folks who were at our table tonight."

"Or were you really fascinated by the comely Miss Nadia Wordell?" Lily posed, arching an eyebrow.

"Well, I did happen to notice her, but only in a dispassionate way."

"You, dispassionate, when it comes to attractive women? Are you trying to make me choke on my drink?"

"All right then, let the record show that I made note of Miss Wordell's visible attributes, but after all, I am a detective, thereby trained to be observant. And as I just said, I really was intrigued, not just by Nadia, but by everyone at the table."

"Overall, they seemed a pretty normal bunch to me," Lily said.

"I am not sure I agree, my love. Let us start with Mr. Mason, for example. The man redefines a mope. He barely spoke a complete sentence all evening, just sat there with his arms folded and with his face set in a glower—not unlike the behavior of the aforementioned Mr. Wordell himself."

"But there is definitely a reason for that, as I suggested to you earlier. Roger Mason feels that he has been undercut and insulted by Wordell's appointment of that advisory board, or whatever he's calling it," Lily said. "After all, Mr. Mason has good credentials, having been the director of two or three art museums up in the New England states."

"Is Mason married?"

"Divorced for many years, which may or may not mean that he's hard to get along with."

"True. But one thing we do know is that the gentleman's psyche has been badly bruised. Does he have to share his misery with a roomful of people who presumably have come to celebrate the new museum? For that matter, why did he bother to show up at all tonight?"

"Perhaps to protect his position with Wordell, however shaky it is, and to keep an eye on that trio of new advisers who he feels are undercutting him."

"One of whom is Faith Richmond, she with the oversize glasses that make her eyes look as big as basketballs," I observed. "Maybe she's trying to be intimidating."

"Faith? Not really," Lily said. "Oh, she can be strong-minded, but then, as the biographer of several nineteenth- and twentieth-century artists, she has never been shy about stating her opinions, not all of them positive, regarding their work. And her books have been generally well received in the arts community, or so I have been told."

"If not necessarily by the artists she writes about?"

Lily laughed. "Faith has never been one to let criticism faze her. I heard a talk she gave at a luncheon a couple of years ago in which she told us that one cubist painter she had been critical of in her book about him was so upset that he mailed her a caricature of herself in which those magnified eyes you referred to were covered by a blindfold. The caption read 'Do not put your *Faith* in a blind woman.' "

"At least the painter has a sense of humor."

"So does Faith, for that matter," Lily said. "Her response to his drawing of her was a sketch she did and mailed to him, with copies sent to the newspapers' arts critics. In it, he was depicted as a robot—all square corners as befits cubism—with a caption reading 'Hardly what one would call a well-rounded individual.' That got her some mentions in a couple of the papers."

"Nice to know there's some puckishness in these artsy sorts. I certainly didn't see much of it tonight. Some of the men seemed awfully fawning around Wordell—Wolfe would call them sycophants."

"I must say that being around your boss is doing wonders for your vocabulary, although I did not sense a lot of fawning at the dinner myself."

"What about Henry Banks, who was soothing Wordell by telling him not to take the unctuous master of ceremonies too seriously? Or Tatum, that prof down at NYU, who cozied up to the famous collector, telling him that he was a 'man of mystery' by keeping people guessing as to where his art would go. And that tall drink of water Sterling also jumped in, urging Wordell to respond to the applause with appreciation. I would call all of that fawning."

Lily responded with a sigh. "I feel, my dear Escamillo, that I have made a mistake by dragging you here tonight. I should have learned my lesson by this time. For years, I have hauled you along to all manner of arts events—gallery openings, lectures by and about artists, even that auction where I was fortunate enough to buy a Fernand Léger. And you always went along, albeit I suspect reluctantly. It's clear that you are not comfortable around these people, and I guess that is understandable."

"If I may continue dissecting the assemblage, exactly what was Tatum's role? He is not one of that board of advisers."

"Ah, yes, Boyd," she said. "Besides being a professor of considerable repute at New York University, he, like Faith, is something of a writer in the field of art and art collectors, and for some time now, he has been trying hard to get Arthur Wordell to agree to a biography."

"To be written by Tatum, of course."

"Of course."

"I suppose that would explain at least some of his rather fawning nature," I said as I took a sip of my drink and set it down. "I am sorry to act like such a grouch, my dear, but something just didn't feel right to me tonight. Maybe it's something I ate, although I can hardly complain about the dinner that the Waldorf served us. I hereby promise not to be such a crank."

"Bravo—that's the spirit! Changing the subject slightly, what do you think of the new Guggenheim's architecture?"

"Unusual, to say the least. This guy Wright is famous, from what I've heard over the years, so maybe I have no business being critical of his work."

"You certainly were not critical of his granddaughter when you met her."

"Huh?"

"It was two or three years back, at a party we went to after the New York premiere of that Cecil B. DeMille biblical epic, *The Ten Commandments*. Surely you can't have forgotten the evening."

"I remember that party, all right. It was quite a bash, as I recall. A 'Hollywood Comes to New York' event."

"Then you must remember a fetching actress from that film who was at the party, the one you couldn't take your eyes off, Anne Baxter by name. I seem to recall you spent some time talking to her in close quarters."

"I was just being . . . social."

"Very social, I would say, and I know that you can't help being who you are. Anyway, she is the granddaughter of the great architect himself. Artistic talent must run in the family."

"It must. Did I really seem enchanted by the lady?"

"I can't believe you have forgotten. I admit to being jealous of her for a full minute, but then my better self took over. Let us order another drink," Lily said, covering my hand with hers, "and we'll talk about something other than the comely Miss Baxter, like whether the Rangers have any chance whatever to win that elusive Stanley Cup this season."

CHAPTER 3

For at least two weeks after that dinner at the Waldorf, I gave no thought whatever to the Guggenheim Museum, Arthur Wordell, Frank Lloyd Wright, Anne Baxter, and the worlds of the fine arts and architecture in general. Maybe Lily was right that I was so far out of my element in that milieu that it had turned me into a misanthrope. During those days, I was busy working with Wolfe to crack the case of an Upper West Side widow's missing federal bearer bonds.

Mrs. Eleanora Winston, who lived in splendor in one of those elaborate nineteenth-century co-op palaces that line Central Park West, had always been careless with money, probably because she had always had so much of it, courtesy of her late husband from Pittsburgh, who had made it big in the steel business.

One day, the octogenarian noticed that her bonds were missing, and she had no idea when she had last seen them. The police were not interested in the case, so one of Mrs. Winston's daughters hired Wolfe, and by extension, me, to locate those missing securities, which added up to hundreds of thousands of dollars.

From the start, it seemed obvious to us that this had to be an inside job, despite the old woman's contention that none of her offspring or their spouses could possibly have filched the bonds. No tradesman had set foot in the apartment in nearly a year, and the only domestic help was a maid nearly as old as her employer and who had been on the job for nearly three decades.

That left two sons, their wives, two daughters, and their husbands. Eight suspects in all, three of whom—two sons and a son-in-law—had what could euphemistically be described as "money problems."

Through some grilling, first by me and then by Wolfe, we bore in on the trio, and ironically, the husband of the woman who hired us turned out to be the sticky-fingered one.

In a piece of good news for the widow, he had not cashed in the bonds, which got returned to her intact. In a second piece of good news, at least for the thief, his mother-in-law did not press charges. As the best news of all, Wolfe got paid in full for his—and my—work.

So, comfortable in the knowledge that our bank balance was once more at what I consider an adequate level, I sat at my desk in the office on a sunny morning nursing coffee after having been served Canadian bacon, an apricot omelet, and blueberry muffins by Fritz Brenner at my little table in the kitchen.

The phone rang, which I answered in the usual way during working hours: "Nero Wolfe's office, Archie Goodwin speaking."

It was Lily. "Do you have the radio turned on this morning, Escamillo?"

I said no and could hear her draw in air. "Arthur Wordell

died sometime last night. He fell to the ground from his office in Midtown."

"Are there any other details in the radio report?"

"None. It said that the police are investigating."

"As of course they would be. I think I'll make a call."

"Let me guess: you are going to telephone a certain Mr. Cohen at a certain metropolitan New York daily newspaper."

"As a mind reader, you are second to none."

"It has often been said," Lily said. "Let me know what you learn."

I wasn't sure why I cared about the circumstances of Wordell's death, other than out of curiosity, given that I had recently met the man. But then, I am a detective, and that makes me inquisitive by definition. Using a number that I knew by heart, I dialed Lon Cohen at the *Gazette* and got the usual gruff "Yeah?" after one ring.

"I haven't heard one word from you since our last poker game," Lon said after I had identified myself. "Are you sore about that big pot I won on that bluff?"

"I was bluffing, too, and my guess is that you had the better hand anyway."

"You will never know. Okay, just what's on your mind?"

"I'm wondering what you've heard regarding Arthur Wordell's demise."

"How is it that whenever there's a high-profile death in this city that is the least bit mysterious, you and your boss get curious about it?"

"Explain that 'least bit mysterious' part," I asked.

"All we know right now is that Wordell fell out of a window in his twentieth-floor office sometime after nine last night. What's left of him was lying in a parking lot that borders three buildings in the middle of a block just east of Seventh Avenue and three blocks north of Times Square. He was found about six this morning by a parking lot attendant coming on duty."

"There were no eyewitnesses?"

"None. One man we spoke to, who also had talked to the cops, works as an accountant in a building that faces Wordell's across that parking lot. He says Wordell—whose name he didn't know until today—had a habit of throwing open his window, sitting on the sill with his legs dangling on the outside, and gazing at that part of the city he could see. The accountant said Wordell sometimes sat there for an hour or more, just staring and taking deep breaths."

"So it's possible that he could have been doing that last night and slipped?"

"Of course it's possible. Hey—wait a minute, what is your interest in all this, gumshoe? Tell your old uncle Lon just what's going on here. Do you have yourselves a client?"

"We do not, Uncle Lon. Just chalk it up to my general interest in what seem to be unexplained deaths."

"Uh-huh. If that's your story, by all means stick with it. Now if you will excuse me, we're getting close to the deadline on our first edition."

"Before you go, what are the police saying about this?"

"Not much. They don't seem to think it's a suicide. Right now, they appear to be going with the accidental death theory. Now I've really gotta go."

Ninety minutes later, I checked my watch and saw that it was time for our delivery of the *Gazette*'s first edition. Sure enough, it was out on the stoop. I brought it in and read the page one story headlined "Noted Art Collector Found Dead After a Fall." The story, which had to have been put together quickly, added nothing to what Lon had told me. An unnamed police spokesman was quoted as saying, "We are looking into the death and will release more information if and when it becomes available."

I laid the paper aside and opened the morning mail, then set to typing the letters Wolfe had dictated yesterday. I finished the last one just as he walked into the office at 11:03 after his two-hour morning session with the orchids up in the plant rooms on the roof.

"Did you sleep well, Archie?" he asked as usual as he put a raceme of yellow-and-brown *Oncidium* in the vase on his desk, sat, and rang for beer. I answered in the affirmative and turned to face him.

"You recall my mentioning Arthur Wordell."

"The gentleman at whose table you sat during that museum dinner," Wolfe replied as Fritz brought in a tray with two bottles of beer and a chilled stein and set it before him. "You said you were filled with an unease you could not articulate that night."

I shrugged. "Maybe."

"Not maybe. As I have said before, despite your faults, and they are legion, you are possessed with a sense of prescience. Are you about to tell me that quality has been borne out in some way involving Mr. Wordell?"

"I suppose that it might be," I said, handing him the *Gazette* and pointing at the article. "Wordell was found dead in a Midtown parking lot this morning. He had fallen twenty stories sometime in the night, apparently from the sill of an open window in his office where he often sat."

"Indeed," Wolfe responded blandly, scanning the article and popping the cap off one of his beer bottles.

I then filled him in on my conversation with Lon. "So Wordell was somewhat screwy, preferring to sit on that windowsill and watching what he could see and hear of the city below him," I concluded. "He did it several nights a week. It is possible he lost his balance up there and . . ."

Wolfe took a healthy swig of beer and flipped through the mail I had stacked on his desk blotter.

"Do you have any thoughts about Wordell's plunge?" I asked.

"No, should I?" Wolfe asked. "Apparently the police attribute the death to carelessness on the gentleman's part. Do you entertain another theory?"

"I guess not at the moment."

Wolfe picked up his current book, *Only in America*, by Harry Golden, and opened it, signaling that there would be no further discussion at present regarding the death of Arthur Wordell.

CHAPTER 4

The next morning, Lily Rowan and I left on a two-week vacation to the Caribbean. This venture of ours had been planned for some time, with Wolfe's approval. After all, the brownstone's finances were relatively robust, and no cases loomed on our horizon. Besides, Wolfe and I needed time apart occasionally because my badgering of him—a large part of the reason I was hired way back when—tended to get on his nerves. And in truth, he gets on my nerves as well.

Adding to the tension between us was a pair of ongoing arguments: I had been after Wolfe to get our aged Heron sedan replaced with a new model, and he was after me to scrap my old clickety-clack typewriter that irritated him and get one of the new noiseless models that were being advertised in the newspapers. Neither of us had budged, however, and this holiday was well timed.

Those days away from New York were a tonic for both Lily and me—swimming, scuba diving, tennis, dancing on a moonlit terrace, one round of golf on a challenging course—I won, but not by much—wonderful meals (if not always quite up to Fritz's standards), and just plain relaxing. We got home on a flight from San Juan on a Tuesday morning, and it was just after eleven when I rang the front doorbell of the brownstone, using the two longs, three shorts signal Fritz would recognize.

He opened the door with a grin and took my luggage. "Welcome home. I hope you and Miss Rowan enjoyed yourselves in the sunshine," he said with the slightest of bows.

"We really did," I replied and walked down the hall, surprised to see that the office door was closed. I threw a questioning look at Fritz, who said, "Mr. Wolfe has two people in there with him, but he said to let you in if you got home while they were meeting. In fact, they just got started a few minutes ago."

Realizing the vacation had officially ended, I opened the door and found myself looking at two familiar faces—three if you count Wolfe's. In the red leather chair, which is often reserved for a client, sat a shyly smiling Nadia Wordell, and in one of the yellow chairs reclined Wolfe's longtime friend and fellow orchid fancier Lewis Hewitt.

"Ah, Archie, welcome back," Wolfe said in a tone filled with uncharacteristic bonhomie. "I trust you and Miss Rowan had an enjoyable sojourn."

After I answered with a nod and a few words and sat at my desk for the first time in fourteen days, Wolfe pushed on.

"You of course know both of our guests. During your absence, Mr. Hewitt called me on behalf of Miss Wordell, who happens to be his goddaughter. She strongly feels her father was pushed to his death from his office in Midtown and has asked that we conduct an investigation, as the police seem inclined to view his demise as misadventure. I am not yet ready to undertake such a project and have invited her here to make her case. I am glad you are present to help in our making a decision."

Okay, let the record show that Wolfe was grandstanding for the benefit of our guests, particularly Nadia. The idea that I would be an integral part of any major decision-making process in the brownstone was patently absurd, but she did not know that. I tried my best to look important.

"When you came in," Wolfe said, turning toward me, "I was about to ask Miss Wordell to state her reasons for believing her father was pushed from that windowsill. You may present your case, madam."

Nadia straightened up and licked her lips. "First, I want to dismiss once and for all any idea that my father might have committed suicide. That is simply ludicrous. He was eccentric and unpredictable, no question about that, but he enjoyed life far too much to want to end it. And as to his accidentally falling from a windowsill in his office, I find that also to be utter nonsense.

"He had been perching there frequently for years, and as far as I was able to tell, he had lost none of his mental competence or his agility. Daddy did exercises every day at home, and his doctor recently said he had the constitution of someone at least twenty years younger."

"Why did Mr. Wordell make it a habit to sit in that window opening hundreds of feet above the ground?" Wolfe asked.

"He always said that he loved the sights and sounds—and smells—of the city, and from that vantage point, he could get a sampling of all three," Nadia said, shaking her head.

"Because the other buildings on that block were shorter than his, he had views onto the street where he could see traffic, pedestrians, delicatessens, neon signs, and the general of bustle of Midtown, which he often said energized him," she continued.

"Did he spend time in that office every day?"

"No, not at all, maybe two or three times a week or so. It is a very drab, unadorned two-room space, and other than his love of looking out on what he liked to call 'my city,' I could never understand for the life of me why he bothered to keep that space," his daughter said. "I am sure he got far more work done in his study at home on the Upper East Side than in that dumpy old building."

Wolfe drank beer and set his glass down. "Did he have an office staff?"

"Only one elderly woman—that is to say, she is close to my father's age—Mabel Courtney. As far as I was able to tell, she was mostly there to answer what few calls my father got at that number. Oh, she did also type some correspondence for him on an ancient Smith Corona model that looked like it should be on display in the Smithsonian."

"How often did the Courtney woman work for him?"

"Usually no more than a couple of times a week. Daddy would usually call her the day before he was going to be in that office, and she would show up. Oh, and she also sometimes went to his town house on the Upper East Side to take dictation as well. I don't know how they had originally met, but she seemed very devoted to him, possessive in a platonic way, I mean. I didn't much care for the woman; she was fussy and cranky toward everyone except Daddy. It was obvious she didn't like me, and whenever I went to see him when she was present, I could tell she felt I was intruding."

"Does that Midtown building have a security system?" I put in.

"Hah! Even though it's more than twenty stories high, it seems like something out of another era," Nadia said. "The creaky, open-cage elevators look like Mr. Otis must have designed them himself. And judging by the empty spaces on the directory in that threadbare lobby, at least half the building is unoccupied. There are never guards on duty and there's no reception person or guard manning the lobby, which is in desperate need of a paint job. Maybe that's why the rents are so low."

"So people are likely to come and go without any record of them?"

"That's right, Mr. Goodwin. If I were in charge of the city, I would condemn the structure today."

"Miss Wordell, do you care to nominate anyone as a potential murderer?" Wolfe asked.

She shook her head slowly and chewed on her lower lip. "I know Daddy was not popular with a lot of people. He could be gruff, rude, and plainspoken. He didn't seem to care what people thought of him, and I am sure he must have made enemies whom I know nothing about."

"How would you describe his relationship with your mother?" Wolfe asked.

She frowned. "In case you did not know, Alexis and I aren't related by blood. My own mother died when I was twelve, and Daddy remarried about three years later. I never spent a lot of time around Alexis—by design. Most of the time they were living together, I was in boarding school and then away at a university in Massachusetts, which was just fine with me."

"Is that by way of suggesting there was animus between you and your father's second wife?"

That brought the hint of a smile. "That is a fair statement, Mr. Wolfe. Alexis Evans Farrell Wordell is a very strong-willed, acerbic, and opinionated woman. She is difficult to like."

"Traits also possessed by your father?"

Now the smile was more than a hint, and it was accompanied by a nod. "Your point is well taken. Perhaps that was why their marriage seemed like it was doomed from the start, and they separated several years ago. They were just too much alike in too many ways. I never understood what Daddy saw in her, but then, it was hardly for me to judge—I wasn't marrying the woman."

"With your father's death, what is the status of what I understand to be an extremely valuable collection of art?"

"That is a question the newspapers already have been asking. The incredible fact is that Daddy died without any will that we are aware of. Both our lawyer and I had been begging him to draw one up for years, but he always brushed us off. It was like he felt he was going to live for . . . well, forever.

"We've gone through all his papers, and there is no sign whatever of a will. As to the status of the collection, I really don't know right now. But what I do know is that Alexis would love to get hold of Daddy's art, or at least a large part of it."

"Is the woman financially strapped?"

"Strapped!" Nadia made a face and sniffed. "Far from it. She had money from her first marriage, to a man named Farrell who made his big bundle in the lumber business up in the Pacific Northwest. And I happen to know that Daddy was very generous to her in their financial settlements. But she is one of those people who feel that they never have enough."

"Why did they not divorce?" Wolfe asked.

"He wanted one, but she refused to grant it. She is Catholic, more or less, probably less than more, and she said she did not want a divorce to taint her standing in the church, whatever that means. Her first husband had died of a heart attack."

"Is she aware that your father died intestate?"

"That is certainly possible. They split up four . . . no, it's just about five years ago now, and of course Alexis probably would have known at the time that he hadn't drawn up a will. The

newspapers have asked both our lawyer and me about the exis-
tence of a will, and we have consistently refused to comment,
so as far as I am aware, no one outside of a small circle knows
for sure."

I could tell Wolfe was getting bored and thinking about
lunch, which I later learned was to be baked scallops and endive
salad. "Do you believe his estranged wife to be responsible in
any way for your father's death?"

"I . . . no!" Nadia said, jerking upright in her chair. "It's true
that I have never liked Alexis, but I can't imagine her under
any circumstances having something to do with . . . with what
happened."

"I will ask you once more, Miss Wordell: Can you conceive
of any individual who might have killed your father?"

She drew in air and let it out audibly. "That is a very difficult
question."

"Yet you propose hiring me to identify a murderer?"

"If I named someone, I couldn't bear it if I were wrong," she
said, almost in tears.

"I assure you, madam, that anything said between me and
a client in this room remains confidential. I believe I can speak
also for Mr. Hewitt and Mr. Goodwin." We both nodded.

Nadia pulled herself together. "I'm sorry, but I am not prepared to point a finger at anyone."

"Do you have any thoughts on the matter?" Wolfe asked,
turning to Lewis Hewitt.

"No, only that I have known Nadia since the day she was
born, and I have never seen her surer of anything than she is
that her father did not die accidentally."

"Just so. And now if you both will excuse me, I have another
engagement to attend to," Wolfe said, rising and walking out of
the office.

"Thank you both for coming," I told Hewitt and Nadia. "Mr. Wolfe or I will be getting back to you on where we go from here." After I saw them out and bolted the front door, I went to the kitchen, where Wolfe and Fritz were in a heated discussion involving the use of chives.

"Very cute," I told my boss, "very cute indeed. We usually get a case because I goad you into taking it. And here, with me away on some Caribbean sandy beach with a tall, cool drink and a lovely woman, you up and land one all by yourself. I congratulate you on a nice job."

"I have committed to nothing!" Wolfe barked.

"Well, you are sure off to a good start in the direction of being committed. If I didn't know any better, I would think maybe you were once again in the debt of your old friend Lewis Hewitt. Oh, wait, you *are* in Mr. Hewitt's debt," I said, slapping my forehead in mock surprise. "I almost forgot that last month he invited you to dinner with him and that famous orchid grower from Florida you had been wanting to meet for years. And you also got an orchid you coveted from that man down south."

Wolfe glowered at me. "Are you through?"

"I suppose I am. Oh, and on that matter of chives the two of you were kicking around when I walked in, I hereby cast my vote with Fritz. One of my firm principles is that it's never a good idea to argue with the hand that feeds me."

CHAPTER 5

After finishing our meal of baked scallops followed by Fritz's signature cherry cobbler, we sat in the office with coffee. Because cases—even potential ones—are never discussed in the dining room, Wolfe at lunch chose to hold forth on why the Founding Fathers had created the electoral college. As is often the case, my contribution to the conversation was to nod, chew, and throw in the occasional question to show that I was listening.

"All right, so my brain is filled with information on how our elections are supposed to work," I told him. "With that accomplished, should we discuss Miss Wordell's request that we look into her father's death?"

Wolfe set his cup down and pursed his lips. He has never liked the idea of going to work, and this was to be no exception.

"You and Miss Rowan dined at the Waldorf with Mr. Wordell, his daughter, and all those acquaintances of his. I recall how unsettled you were when you returned from the dinner, although at the time, you did not go into specifics about the individuals who were present."

"Are you suggesting one of them might have helped him out of that twentieth-floor window?"

"I am suggesting nothing, merely seeking information. Miss Wordell certainly was not able, or not willing, to nominate anyone who might want to harm her father, yet she seems firm in her belief that he was pushed to his death."

"Yeah, she gave us nothing whatever to go on. I'm a little surprised that Hewitt brought her here, given her lack of ideas. So now what?"

"Give me your thoughts about those at the table."

Wolfe was well aware of my ability to repeat long conversations verbatim, and also to deliver concise descriptions and opinions regarding individuals. I started in, going around the table and giving my thumbnail sketches of each of the guests.

"It seems clear that no one among this assemblage overly impressed you, with the possible exception of Miss Wordell," Wolfe said.

"Agreed." I then proceeded to get more specific about my tablemates. "I will start with Roger Mason, because if Wordell really did get bumped off, this guy might have felt that he had a reason for shoving the old guy off that twentieth-floor window perch of his.

"As Lily spelled it out to me, Wordell had appointed Mason to be the curator of his art collection two or three years earlier. Apparently, that setup worked out okay for a while, but Mason, in spite of his strong background as a top dog at some New England art museums, is highly opinionated and contentious— which sounds a lot like Wordell himself.

"The collector apparently got tired of Mason's arrogance and haughtiness—I think I'm using that word right. Mason eventually had come to feel that the collection belonged to him."

"You are employing haughtiness correctly," Wolfe remarked, pushing the button as a signal to Fritz to bring beer and nodding for me to continue.

"I was struck at the Waldorf dinner by Mason's behavior. His face was set in what seemed to be a permanent pout. He barely spoke all evening and almost never looked at anyone else. I later learned from Lily that he was still fuming over Wordell's recent decision to appoint what he called a board of advisers—three people, all of whom seem to be well versed in the world of fine art—to help him decide the future of his collection. And it had to gall Mason that each of them was right there at the table that night as reminders of his fall from grace."

"Without doubt. No one among us wants to be reminded of a real or imagined failure."

"I am sure Mason would rather not have wanted to be there, but as Lily has pointed out, he felt he had to protect his position."

"Miss Rowan is most perspicacious," Wolfe said. "Do you have anything more to add about the beleaguered Mr. Mason?"

"Nope. I've unloaded everything I have on him, other than a feeling that I would not want to spend more than five minutes in his presence."

"Tell me your impressions about those three who form Mr. Wordell's board of counselors."

"Okay, let us start with Henry Banks, who is probably in his late fifties and who, like Mason, has a background as a curator. Lily told me he had been an adviser to a couple of wealthy collectors in the New York suburbs. He's short, portly, and balding, the hail-fellow-well-met type, and, like others around that table, he seemed intent on buttering up Arthur Wordell. When that self-satisfied master of ceremonies prematurely suggested that Wordell was to give his collection to the Guggenheim, the old man almost popped his cork, threatening to walk out. First Nadia talked her father into staying, and then Banks really laid on the flattery, trying with limited success to calm Wordell down. It was a classic example of a toady in action."

"Reprehensible," Wolfe muttered.

"Yeah, but Banks was hardly alone in the groveling act. Emory Sterling, who I would describe as courtly and seventy-ish, also played the lackey very well."

"Mr. Sterling's position?"

"He is the longtime publisher of a magazine called *Art & Artists* and according to Lily is highly respected in the rarefied world of the fine arts. He cuts quite a figure and is aware of it. When Wordell bristled after the applause he got but didn't want, Sterling gave him some stroking by telling him the audience was just showing their appreciation for his role as a collector."

"Which did not mollify Mr. Wordell," Wolfe stated.

"Not in the least. He just scowled, which he did a lot of that evening. The third member of the advisory group is Faith Richmond, probably around fifty, with glasses that make her eyes look like automobile headlights set to the high beam. She is a biographer of nineteenth- and twentieth-century artists and apparently is well thought of and knowledgeable, according to Lily.

"The Richmond woman is reserved, almost to the point of iciness, and she is known to be highly opinionated. She too fawned over Wordell, telling him how wonderful he was and hoping that he would favor the new museum with his collection."

Wolfe made a face, which he often does when a woman enters into the conversation. I ignored him and pushed on. "Then there is Boyd Tatum, not on the advisory board but a professor who teaches some sort of art courses down at New

York University. He is another of those at the Waldorf dinner who kowtowed to Wordell, gushing that he was a man of mystery and intrigue for not revealing where his collection would end up.

"To be fair, in Tatum's case there was at least one good reason why he should butter up the collector: he, like Faith Richmond, has done biographies of figures in the arts, and he had been trying to persuade Wordell to let him write his biography."

"Did you also learn this from Miss Rowan?" Wolfe asked.

"Guilty as charged. She is what you might call a font of information."

"I might. Do you have anything more to add?"

"Oh, I certainly do, and you are going to love this one—a female artist who goes by the name of Zondra Zagreb." That brought back Wolfe's not-another-woman expression. Before he could speak, I jumped in and described the artist's appearance and her outsize personality. "I will give her this: She was the only one there that night who did not bow down to Wordell like he was some sort of potentate. In fact, she was sassy toward him, and the old grump actually seemed to like it."

"Perhaps he got tired of all that groveling to which he had been subjected."

"A good point. Anyway, that's it; my bag is now empty."

Wolfe drank from his second beer and licked his lips, then dabbed them with one of the fresh handkerchiefs Fritz always keeps in the center drawer of his desk. "It has been some time since Miss Rowan dined with us," he said.

If you think that was a strange remark coming from a man for whom women are an anathema, you need to know that Lily Rowan is the exception that proves the rule. It dates from their first meeting, when almost the first words out of Lily's mouth were "I would love to see your orchids."

From that moment on, she has been a welcome guest in the brownstone, and she has made many trips up to the greenhouse on the roof to admire those ten thousand orchids in the three climate-controlled rooms, with Wolfe playing gracious tour guide. And on numerous occasions, she has left the brownstone with an orchid or two.

"When would you like her to come to dinner?"

"Tonight would be preferable if she entertains no other plans," Wolfe said. "We are having lamb cutlets with gammon and tomatoes, followed by raspberries in sherry cream."

"Well, if she does happen to have other plans, they don't involve me. I will telephone her."

"How nice to hear from you, Escamillo," Lily said. "To what do I owe the pleasure?"

"I believe that it will be a pleasure for you, that is, if you happen to be available. Mr. Wolfe was just saying that it has been a long time since you joined us for dinner. How about tonight?"

"This is very late notice, I must say, but I have to admit that my calendar is clear, and as you know, I have always marveled at Fritz's culinary artistry. What time would you like me to make an appearance?"

"How about seven?"

"How about seven—now that sounds good to me. I will be there. Care to tell me what I should be prepared for?"

"Very fine food, of course, and stimulating dinner table conversation. Beyond that, I can only speculate."

"Aha. Somehow, I have this feeling that I am going to be grilled by your boss. And I believe I can guess what the subject will be."

I also knew what lay behind Wolfe's invitation.

CHAPTER 6

Lily rang the doorbell at seven sharp, and, knowing she would be prompt as she always is, I already was in the foyer awaiting her arrival. I swung open the front door and gave what I felt was a proper bow.

"All that's lacking is a trumpet," Lily chirped, stepping in and giving me a hug and a kiss, which I returned. She wore a gray belted number that showed her contours without overselling them, along with matching pumps and the string of pearls that I had given her two Christmases ago. To say she looked terrific would be an understatement.

We went straight into the dining room, where Wolfe was just getting seated, although he made a half-hearted attempt at rising as we entered. "Miss Rowan," he said with creased cheeks, which for him passes as a smile.

"Mr. Wolfe, thank you so much for the invitation," she said, returning the smile and taking the chair I pulled back for her.

Knowing well my boss's aversion to handshakes, she did not hold out an arm.

As soon as we all were seated, Fritz entered and began serving us. He threw a nod in Lily's direction. Like Wolfe, he is usually uncomfortable when women invade the sacred sanctuary of the brownstone, but also like Wolfe, he makes an exception for Lily, whom he seems always glad to see.

After Fritz poured the wine and we began eating our salads, Wolfe launched into a discourse on the lack of women in elected governmental positions and the reasons for it.

Lily had her own opinions, some of which jibed with Wolfe's while others did not. The result was a lively discussion, with me looking from one of them to the other like a spectator at a tennis match that had extended volleys.

Wolfe clearly was enjoying himself. Lily gave as well as she got, and he liked that. She even gently corrected him regarding the name of a woman who had run for a state senate seat in New York. It was good that he had a sparring partner other than me for a change. And he had chosen the topic well.

After dinner, we retired to the office for coffee, after which Fritz served beer to Wolfe and Remisier cognac to Lily and me. "This is wonderful," she said to Wolfe after taking a sip. "But I really shouldn't be drinking too much of it. I know from Archie just how much Lon Cohen of the *Gazette* loves this nectar, and I would hate to think that I might be using it up."

"Of that you need not worry, Miss Rowan," Wolfe replied. "At the rate it is being consumed—and I include Mr. Cohen as among its consumers—it would take more than two decades to exhaust the supply that resides in our cellar. And I realize that I am guilty of the sin of pride when I say that every bottle of Remisier remaining in the United States now resides within these walls."

"I am indeed impressed," Lily said with a laugh. She was seated in the red leather chair normally reserved for clients. I had placed her there by design, knowing it would give Wolfe a good view of her legs. One of the few things that Nero Wolfe appreciates about women is their legs, assuming they are shapely, and Lily's are indeed shapely.

"I must confess I have an ulterior motive in asking you to come here tonight," Wolfe said to our guest as he took a drink of his beer.

"I assumed you did," Lily replied, arching an eyebrow. "But that did not stop me from accepting the invitation."

"As you may know from Archie, I have been approached by the late Mr. Wordell's daughter to investigate his death. She feels it was not an accident."

Lily nodded, saying nothing.

"Miss Wordell is reluctant, however, to suggest any individual who might have wished her father harm. Archie has given me his impressions of all those who were at the Wordell table at that Waldorf dinner. I would now like to hear your thoughts about said individuals."

"If you have already gotten Archie's slant on these people, I'm not sure that I would be able to add much. He is very thorough in describing people."

"Let us stipulate that he is thorough," Wolfe said. "However, I remain interested in your impressions."

There is nothing quite like having two people discuss you as if you were not present. I resisted making a comment lest I interrupt the flow of their conversation.

"All right," Lily said. "I will do the best that I can. Where would you like me to start?"

"Let us begin with Mr. Wordell himself," Wolfe replied.

"I must confess that I really did not know him all that well.

Most of my impressions of the man came through his daughter, Nadia, whom I have come to consider a good friend. She adored her father, although she was well aware of how dismissive and ornery and arrogant he could be. She once told me she wished he were nicer to others, but she is a realist. 'Daddy will never be one of those warm, grandfatherly types,' she said. 'It is just not in his makeup.' "

"Does that suggest he was prone to making enemies?"

"Oh, I am sure that's possible, even likely," Lily replied with the sweeping gesture of a manicured hand. "As I have learned, there's a ton of jealousy in the arts world, despite its very thin veneer of civility. And this jealousy was particularly intense where Arthur Wordell was concerned. For years, he has been buying up great art all over the world, outbidding both individuals and museums at auctions by throwing outrageous amounts of cash around. When he wanted a piece of art badly enough, no one who was also interested could possibly match him. He had left a good deal of bitterness in his wake."

"Was that bitterness widespread?" Wolfe asked.

"I couldn't say for sure, but Nadia mentioned to me a couple of times that there had been general grumbling about the way her father was behaving. He became known as the 'art hog' in some circles, but he did not seem to care in the least what was being said about him."

"Did his daughter ever mention that he received threats?"

"Not to me, she didn't," Lily said. "She just seemed sad about how he was viewed, and she knew there was nothing she could do about it. She was particularly upset when a British arts magazine carried a piece that called Arthur Wordell 'the prince of greed.' Then a *Gazette* columnist picked up on that article, suggesting that Wordell was driving the price of major paintings into the stratosphere permanently. The columnist referred to Wordell's behavior as 'one man's wreckage.' "

"Yet I gather Mr. Wordell had his admirers, including some of those at his table at the Waldorf dinner," Wolfe observed.

"Admirers? I would not have chosen that word. The people you refer to I would term as 'apple-polishers.' "

"A good phrase, and one that I have used on occasion." Wolfe said. "Would you place yourself in that category?"

Lily threw her head back and laughed. "Known by the company I keep, is that your point? I did of course accept an invitation for Archie and me to sit at the Wordell table, but it was tendered by Nadia, whom I suspect wanted at least one friendly face in that gathering. I cannot say that I have ever been an admirer of Arthur Wordell, far from it, although as a New Yorker, I would definitely like to see his collection go to the Guggenheim so we all could enjoy it here."

"Would you care to enlighten us as to your thoughts about the others around the table? I believe I already have a good idea as to your attitudes toward Miss Wordell and, of course, Mr. Goodwin."

Lily turned in my direction and gave me a wink, then shifted back to Wolfe. "All right, I will tackle Roger Mason first, and with him or with any of the others, if I am repeating things Archie has already told you, just let me know and I will move on to somebody else." Wolfe nodded and Lily cleared her throat after taking another sip of the cognac.

"Mason, as you may be aware, was chosen a few years ago by Arthur Wordell to be the curator of his art. But their relationship turned out to be a stormy one in a fairly short time. There was no question about Mason's credentials. He had been a top administrator at several respected museums in New England and apparently did a good job, from what I have heard. But he is highly opinionated and rigid, and the two had a strained relationship almost from the start. Mason also does not hold his liquor well. At an art gallery cocktail party, he made a clumsy, drunken pass at me and—"

"Why, that two-bit—"

"Enough, Archie," Wolfe said, holding up a palm.

"You needn't worry, Escamillo, I fended him off effectively," Lily said. "It is just as well you weren't there, or things might have gotten violent. Anyway, the point is that the man is both stubborn about his opinions and erratic in his behavior. Wordell finally decided he needed someone other than Mason to advise him about his art, and he put together what he referred to as that board of advisers."

"A move Mr. Mason no doubt resented," Wolfe remarked.

"No doubt whatsoever!" Lily replied. "Nadia told me he tried to quit, but Wordell urged him to stay on as curator. As to why he remained, I really have no idea, since the two were like oil and water. But apparently Wordell felt Mason still was of some use to him. From everything I've seen and heard, though, the tension between them was still there. It's a puzzler to me."

"Would you describe Mr. Mason as one given to violence?"

"I honestly don't know," Lily said. "Roger has never seemed to be a very pleasant individual, to say the least, and when he's been drinking, he gets downright surly and contentious. I suppose he is capable of getting physical, although he isn't terribly large—about five eight and thick around the middle. Hardly what you would call the athletic type."

"But he is certainly taller and heavier than Wordell was, who had the build of a jockey," I remarked.

Lily nodded. "No question. I don't believe I can add anything else regarding Roger Mason."

"Continue with the others who were present at the dinner," Wolfe requested.

"I'm happy to go on, Mr. Wolfe, especially after the wonderful dinner and this heavenly cognac, but I am not sure I'm being of any help to you."

"Neither am I, but we must keep on fishing, or we are sure to come trudging home with nothing whatever in our creel. Proceed, unless you are tired."

"Tired? Not at all. Archie can tell you that I have been known to dance into the small hours of the morning without missing a step. As Archie probably told you, the three members of the Wordell advisory board are Faith Richmond, Henry Banks, and Emory Sterling. All of them are said to be extremely knowledgeable in the world of the arts.

"Taking Faith first, I will start by saying that I have never felt any warmth toward her, and if that sounds catty, such is not my intent. She just seems cold and unfeeling, and I've often found myself wondering just how such a person can be passionate about anything, especially great art.

"But then, Arthur Wordell would be a far better judge of that than me. To her credit, she has written biographies of several late-nineteenth- and early-twentieth-century artists. The one I read, about Cézanne, was thorough and reasonably well written, if somewhat plodding in its style. The reviews of her writing, at least the ones I've seen, have been mixed."

"I gather she gets along well with Mr. Wordell," Wolfe said.

"Yes, as far as I can tell, but that may be because she's so deferential toward him. He seems to need . . ."

"Apple-polishers?" Wolfe prompted.

Lily reacted with a laugh. "Ah, yes, there is that phrase again. I should keep Mr. Roget's thesaurus with me at all times so I can find synonyms. I know how particular you are with words and usage."

"I prefer precise to particular, and as far as I am concerned, apple-polisher is indeed precise in this instance. Do you have any further reflections regarding Miss Richmond?"

"No. I hope I haven't been too hard on her, but I am trying to be objective."

"I would expect nothing less than candor from you," Wolfe responded. "Tell me your thoughts about Mr. Banks."

"Henry has been the curator of several private collections of residents living in some of New York's wealthiest suburbs, and he has been very secretive about the owners and their specific works, but I suppose that is a good thing. He is protecting their privacy, as he should. He is said to be an expert on cubist art, of which there are only a few valuable pieces in the Wordell collection. Henry has always been pleasant when we've met; I suppose you could call him sort of a glad-hander, but he has a reputation for being arrogant and dismissive toward those with whom he disagrees.

"According to Nadia, Henry and her father have not always seen eye to eye, and there has been some shouting between them on occasion. But then, she said he was brought on the advisory board because he is not shy about giving his opinions. All this seems somewhat ironic—I hope I am I using that word correctly—because Banks's relationship to Wordell seems a lot like that of Mason's."

"It would appear that Mr. Wordell did not respond well to those who took issue with him, despite what he might claim," Wolfe said. "Did the clashes lessen Mr. Banks's influence on that board?"

"I really don't know," Lily said. "That's a question Nadia probably would be able to answer. The third member of that board is Emory Sterling, whom I have found to be extremely personable. Very patrician in his bearing—he comes from generations of money—he is the longtime editor and publisher, which is to say owner, of the magazine *Art & Artists*, and in addition to his knowledge in all areas of art, he possesses the tact that would be the envy of a career diplomat. He and his wife live the good life—a duplex on Park Avenue, a home at Palm Beach, and a villa on the French Riviera."

"His tact is an asset that would seem to have held him in good stead with the volatile Mr. Wordell," Wolfe observed.

"I am sure of that, and in fact, I heard that he once was being considered for an ambassadorial position. Nadia told me he was something of a peacemaker, moderating and placating when tempers rose, as they invariably did. He seems unflappable, to use a word that has become all the rage recently."

Wolfe scowled but said nothing. His respect for the language and its integrity left little if any room for words or phrases like "all the rage." Lily went on.

"I can't say that I know Emory that well, but from what I have seen on several occasions, he's a real gentleman, and I do not throw that term around recklessly."

"Would you call him a sycophant?" Wolfe asked.

"No, I definitely would not," she replied. "Most of the time he seemed able to disagree with Arthur Wordell without riling him up, which speaks to that tact I mentioned a moment ago."

"Do you have any idea what will happen now to this troika of advisers and Roger Mason?"

"No, and Nadia, with whom I had lunch yesterday, doesn't know either," Lily said. "Everything is in such a state of flux involving the Wordell collection."

"Other than you and Archie, there were two others at that Waldorf table," Wolfe said, prompting Lily.

"Yes, I was planning to get to them—Boyd Tatum and Zondra Zagreb. Boyd is a professor down in Greenwich Village at NYU, where he has been a professor for years in the fine arts program. And he, like Faith Richmond, has written biographies of people in the world of the arts—not just artists themselves, but other important figures, including collectors. He had approached Arthur Wordell about being the subject of one of his books. I think Arthur was initially somewhat flattered—he did have his vanity—and that may be why Boyd was a guest at the table that night."

"Do you know Mr. Tatum?"

"Not well at all," Lily replied, "although I must say he is an engaging man, apparently a confirmed bachelor and very much the image of what a university professor is supposed to look and act like—somewhat rumpled, avuncular, full of academic anecdotes and literary references. And I have also heard that he's popular on campus and is quite an actor in amateur theatrical groups that are made up of faculty and students."

"Well, he certainly works hard enough to cultivate that professorial image of his," I said. "And he poured it on by playing up to Wordell that night. I thought it was sickening to watch."

"I guess you can tell that Professor Boyd Tatum did not impress our Mr. Goodwin," Lily said to Wolfe.

"As you are well aware, Archie is not a man easily impressed. Do you know if Arthur Wordell agreed to have Mr. Tatum write about him?"

"I don't, and I'm not sure that Nadia does, either. But now it's become moot, of course."

"Tell me about that woman artist," Wolfe said.

"Ah, Zondra Zagreb," Lily replied. "I don't know what Archie has related to you about her, but here are my two cents' worth. She is avant-garde, no question. Those who see her for the first time are invariably shocked: Her hair is done in a crew cut, which is usually dyed in an Easter-egg hue, and she is given to wearing muumuus, large earrings, and big necklaces and bracelets. Her eyes are always heavily made up, and she sports a ring in her nose."

"An attention seeker," Wolfe said.

"I suppose she is, but that is all part of what Zondra sees as her persona. Archie probably told you that the name she goes by is not the one she was born with, which is hardly a surprise. But I believe her art to be genuine. She tends to be brash, but for some reason, Arthur Wordell seemed to like her, or at least he was amused by her, even though her artistic style was not necessarily to his taste. Oh, look at the time!" Lily said, glancing at her wristwatch. "I really should be getting my beauty sleep."

"You have been a most welcome guest," Wolfe said as Lily rose to leave.

"I did not ask to see your orchids tonight," she said, "only because I knew there would not be time. May I have a rain check on that?"

"You may," Wolfe said as I walked Lily to the front door and out onto the street. We walked to the corner of Tenth Avenue, where I flagged a taxi, kissed Lily, and held the door for her to climb in. As the cab pulled away, she blew me another kiss from the back window.

CHAPTER 7

When I got back to the office, Wolfe was about to open his current book, *Baruch: My Own Story* by Bernard Baruch. In one of his limited recent ventures out into the world, he had dined at the same table with Baruch and had been very impressed with the man and his work as an adviser to American presidents.

"Well, you can smirk all you want to," I told Wolfe. "You got a lot more information out of Lily than I was able to give you, as I suspected would be the case."

"Hardly a cause for self-flagellation," he said, "as she knows all these people better than you do."

"Yeah, I figured that's why you invited her here tonight, which was fine by me. Have you decided whether to take on Nadia Wordell as a client?"

"Not yet. I have two assignments for you."

"Shoot."

"First, go to that office in Midtown that Mr. Wordell used and determine whether it yields anything of interest, which I concede to be highly unlikely. Second, visit the woman, Mabel Courtney by name, who functioned as Mr. Wordell's secretary and plumb her knowledge, both of her employer and of his occasional workplace."

Wolfe knew he did not have to tell me how to get a key to that office or to learn how to reach Mabel Courtney. He long ago instructed me to "use your intelligence guided by experience," and I have been doing so ever since with a fair degree of success.

The next morning after breakfast, I called Lily for Nadia's telephone number and got a question: "Does that mean Mr. Wolfe is going to investigate her father's death?"

"It is too soon to tell," was my response, and after signing off, I dialed Nadia Wordell.

"Mr. Goodwin, it is so nice to hear from you. What can I do for you?"

I told her what I needed, learned where she lived, and said I would be at her place in twenty minutes. In fact, it was eighteen minutes later when I stepped out of a taxi in the East Seventies and rang the buzzer of an apartment in a white brick ten-story art deco building with a curved, glass-block wall next to the front entrance.

Nadia was already standing in the doorway of her seventh-floor unit wearing a smile and a blue dress when I got there. "Please come in. May I offer you a cup of coffee? I just brewed a pot."

"Yes, I will take you up on that offer, and I drink it black, thanks," I said as I stepped into a good-sized living room that looked like it had been lifted off the pages of a glossy home decorating magazine.

"You have a very nice setup here," I told her, taking a seat on a cream-colored sofa and looking around.

"Thank you," Nadia said, returning from the kitchen and placing a full cup on the end table next to me. "A good friend of mine is an interior decorator, and she was very helpful when I moved in here just over two years ago. I have the key to that dumpy old office Daddy used, although I can't imagine you'll find anything there that will be of any use."

"It's highly possible that you're right about that. Did he keep any of his paperwork in 'that dumpy old office'?"

"Oh, yes, I was about to mention it. He had three filing cabinet drawers full of correspondence, which I pulled out and had moved to Daddy's place on the Upper East Side. I haven't looked at any of the material, or at the files of his that were already in the brownstone, for that matter, other than to determine that there was no will in any of the papers. Would you like to look at what's there?"

"I may at some point. Hang on to everything. I assume that the police visited that Midtown location."

"Yes. An officer, a lieutenant whose name I forget, called and asked me to accompany him to those twentieth-floor rooms. But he spent very little time there, giving the place only a cursory look. The reason, of course, was that the police wrote off what happened as either an accident or suicide—both of which are absurd. Although in their defense, there didn't seem to be much to see in those dingy rooms.

"Oh, and I have the phone number and address of Mabel Courtney," she said, handing me a sheet of paper, "although I can't believe that she'll be very useful. You will probably find her suspicious and very guarded. She is a spinster and was very protective of Daddy, to the point of obsession."

"Was she capable of pushing him off that windowsill?"

Nadia took a deep breath and chewed on her lower lip yet again. "I . . . really can't imagine such a thing. I never liked her, but I can't believe that she would do anything like that."

"Obsessive people sometimes do surprising things," I said. "I'll be interested in talking to her."

"Assuming that she will see you, Mr. Goodwin."

"Why don't you call me Archie?"

"All right, I will, but only if you call me Nadia. Lily has said very nice things about you."

"I am happy to hear that, of course. She and I go back a long way."

"Well, I think both of you are very fortunate," Nadia said, her cheeks coloring. "Maybe someday, I'll have . . ." She let it trail off, and I was not about to encourage her to continue.

The old building in Midtown did indeed have a shabby, unadorned lobby, as I had been told. Judging by the directory, more than half the space in the structure was vacant. I had surely walked along this block dozens of times over the years, but the place never made an impression on me, probably because there were no stores at street level. I did, however, have a vague recollection that a barbershop had once been on the first floor, but its dirty windows looked like they had long ago been covered over with brown paper.

I rode up alone to the twentieth floor in a creaky, open-cage self-service elevator that made squeaking sounds. The dark wood door to suite 2016 had a pebbled glass window that allowed light but not sight. I opened the door with Nadia's key and went into the stark anteroom where Mabel Courtney had done her typing. I knew that, trained detective as I am, because the old Smith Corona upright that Nadia had referred to still sat on a battered wooden desk. The only other pieces of furniture in the windowless room were a chair on wheels and a three-drawer filing cabinet. All its drawers had been emptied by Nadia, as she had mentioned.

A door, which was open, led to the inner sanctum, where Arthur Wordell must have sat behind another equally battered wooden desk and dictated letters to Mabel Courtney. This space was as bare as the anteroom, the major difference being that it had a window—*the* window. I walked over to it and saw that slice of Midtown Wordell had so often gazed upon. I looked down onto the parking lot where he died, now jammed with cars packed tightly together. In a gap between two shorter buildings to the south, I could see the marquee of a legitimate theater and the neon sign advertising an Italian restaurant, whose garlic aroma I swear I could smell, even two hundred feet up, while to the west and south, the lights of Times Square cut through the morning fog on this overcast day.

I pulled up the window and studied the wooden sill where Wordell had spent so much time. It was narrow, but then so was he, and he must have found a way to perch there comfortably and daydream or do whatever it was that captivated him in this mundane urban setting.

How could a man with so much money and such an appreciation for great art rent such a dump and spend so much of his time gazing at so very little? He was eccentric, but then so is my boss, and many of his actions continue to baffle me, even after all these years. But Wolfe is an amateur eccentric compared to Wordell. I spent a few more minutes pacing around the two drab rooms and peering into corners with my penlight, somehow expecting to find an answer to what happened that night Wordell went out and down onto the parking lot.

But no clues presented themselves, and just where would they hide, anyway? Other than the few chairs and desks and some balls of dust in the corners, the joint was as bare and as uninteresting as Old Mother Hubbard's cupboard.

The fatal windowsill had scratches on its wooden surface, but they looked like they had been there for ages. I realized that spending any more time in the place was a fool's errand, and I moved toward the hall door, which I had left ajar, when a burly, bald, and mooselike specimen in dirty coveralls and needing a shave pushed his way in and gave me a glare that apparently was meant to scare me.

"What in the hell are you doing here, pal?" he snorted, rubbing his hand across a face that needed a shave. "This space is not for rent. Just how did you get in, that's what I'd like to know?"

"With this key," I told him, holding it up. "Who are you?"

"I should be asking that question, since I happen to work for the building management. Now get the hell out," the moose said.

"I will leave when I am ready to leave and not before," I told him.

"You will leave right now, pal," he said, stepping forward and giving me a shove in the chest with a beefy hand the size of a small skillet.

As I staggered back, the moose delivered a right in the general direction of my face, but he was too slow by a good half second, which can be forever in a slugfest. I dodged his fist, which grazed my cheek, and I delivered a right of my own to his stomach, which turned out to be an Achilles's heel, so to speak. He collapsed like a tent that had been pitched by tenderfoot campers and cursed, clutching his midsection with both hands, doubling over, and dropping to the floor.

"If you're going to insist on playing games, you had better know just who you are playing against, *pal*," I said, stepping over his writhing and retching body and walking out of the dismal rooms once occupied by Arthur Wordell and his sometime secretary, whom I soon would meet.

CHAPTER 8

I had come via the open-cage elevator, and once again I found myself as its sole passenger. If this building had ever had glory days, which was questionable, they had long since passed.

Out on the street, I consulted the sheet Nadia had given me and found that Mabel Courtney lived in the Hell's Kitchen neighborhood, only a few blocks west and north. After a ten-minute walk, I located her building, a four-story brick walk-up on Ninth Avenue just south of Fiftieth Street that had a Chinese restaurant, a bakery, a deli, and an Irish bar on the street level.

I found the door to the apartments and pushed the buzzer under a card that read COURTNEY 3D. "Yes, what is it?" came a hoarse, high-pitched voice punctuated by a cough.

"I am here to talk about Mr. Wordell's death," I said into the squawk box.

"And who are you?"

"Someone who wants justice for Arthur Wordell."

"You will have to identify yourself," the voice demanded.

"My name is Archie Goodwin, and I am a private investigator licensed by the state of New York and working for Nero Wolfe. I came here at the suggestion of Nadia Wordell, who said she felt you would want to see me."

A long pause, and then "All right," followed by a click that released the door leading to the stairway. I climbed two flights of squeaking wooden steps to the third-floor landing and peered along the dimly lit hall, noticing a door about halfway down that appeared to be opened a crack. As I walked toward it, I could see part of a face through the narrow slit.

"Don't come any closer, I want to look at you," a woman said. "And I have the chain on, so you are not getting in until—or if—I let you."

"All right," I told her, holding out my private detective's license with my mug shot. "I come in peace."

She replied with a snort and pulled the door open. Mabel Courtney looked pretty much as had I expected, seventyish, with a wrinkled, angular face, long, straight nose, thin lips, penetrating eyes behind bifocals set halfway down that nose, and a narrow frame that barely escaped being bony. Her yellow, patterned housedress did her appearance no favors.

"Well, don't just stand there like a ninny, come on inside or I'll change my mind and send you packing so fast that you won't know what hit you," she said.

"Thank you," I told her as I stepped into a small, neat living room with a plaid davenport, two straight-backed chairs, two floor lamps with unmatched shades, and a pair of lace-curtained windows that looked out on bustling Ninth Avenue. "Have a seat anywhere. I suppose you are expecting coffee," she said sharply.

"Not necessarily, I—"

"For heaven's sake, don't dither. I already have a pot on, so it's no bother at all. You look like the type who takes it black."

"I am, and—"

"That's enough. A simple yes would have been quite sufficient," Mabel snapped, marching out of the room, presumably in the direction of the kitchen.

Within seconds, she came back with cups of coffee for each of us. I parked on the davenport while she sat primly in a straight-backed chair at right angles to me. "Now, tell me exactly why it is that you are here, Mr. . . . Goodwin, is it?"

"Yes. As you probably know, Nadia Wordell is convinced that her father was pushed to his death."

She nodded curtly. "The fact is, Nadia is something of a shrinking violet, as far as I am concerned, although I have no doubt that she loved her father very much."

"Do you think Mr. Wordell was murdered?"

"I may not be as sure as Nadia seems to be according to you, but it would not totally surprise me. Arthur did not suffer fools gladly, as Saint Paul wrote in Second Corinthians. He was very plainspoken, and he did not care a whit if he offended someone."

"That would hardly seem to be grounds for murder," I observed.

"That has occurred to me as well," she said. "But like Nadia, I have trouble believing that Arthur slipped off that ledge. I know he had perched in that spot countless times over the six years I had been working for him. He would dictate to me for an hour or more, and when he was done, I would type up his correspondence while he went to the window, sat on the sill, and looked out. The city fascinated him, even though I was never in the least impressed by that view from his window. But let us face it, Mr. Goodwin, Arthur was a singular individual, the most interesting—and cantankerous—person I ever came across."

"You and Nadia seem to be in agreement that he would not have lost his balance. What about suicide?"

"Never!" she said, dismissing the idea with a slicing motion of her hand. "He had far too big an ego to consider killing himself. Besides, he was enjoying the stir that he had created by keeping people guessing as to whether his art would end up in the new Guggenheim place."

"How often did you work for him?"

"Usually about twice a week, sometimes three times," she said. "He would call me when he had several letters to dictate. I got the job in the first place by answering a newspaper ad for a typist. I reported to that old office, and he gave me what might laughingly be called a test. He dictated two short letters, I typed them without error, and he hired me on the spot. I might add that he paid me very well, although the exact figure is of no concern whatever to you."

"Did you always work for him in that twentieth-floor space in Midtown?"

"No, there were times when he asked me to come to his home up in the East Eighties, especially when the weather was bad. He didn't like to sit on that windowsill in the rain or, heaven help us, the snow, so at least he had some sense regarding that ridiculous habit of his."

"Did he get many visitors when you were working?"

"Too many, in my opinion. One of the countless things wrong with that tired old building was that there was no control whatever as to who could come in. The lobby did not have a guard or anybody else on duty, so every Tom, Dick, or Harry could waltz in and go anywhere they pleased. But then, even at his home, he would stop his dictating whenever anyone dropped by. If I were him, I would have insisted that people make appointments to meet him, but that wasn't my place."

"Who would waltz in to see Mr. Wordell?"

"Nadia, for one. She used to drop by occasionally, ostensibly to see her father. She never liked me—that was obvious to me—and I sensed she thought I wanted to marry Arthur, which was patently absurd. Whenever she stopped by, I felt the real reason was that she wanted to check up on me."

"Who else dropped in?"

"Where to start? Some days it seemed like a parade. A lot of people wanted to curry favor with Arthur, and he was easily accessible in that old building. I screwed up my courage once and told him it would be better if we worked more often at his home, where we would at least have some privacy and a butler to answer the door. But he didn't appear to mind the constant interruptions. In fact, he sometimes seemed to relish them."

"Do you have names?"

"Of course I do—I am not senile, Mr. Goodwin!" Mabel Courtney huffed as she took a sip of coffee. "There was that Mason, he probably came the most often."

"Roger Mason?"

"That's the one, usually very whiny. I tried not to eavesdrop on their conversations, but it was hard not to, even when they went into the other room and closed the connecting door. Mason, who looked underfed, was always complaining about something or someone. He was particularly upset over those three people who formed that advisory board to give Arthur their opinions about his collection."

"Did Wordell and Mason argue a lot?"

She nodded. "Sometimes they would go into the other room, the one with the window, and as I said, they would close the door. I could hear them going at it, though, and when they came back out, they both looked like they were ready to chew nails, as my father used to say."

"Did Wordell ever talk to you about his relationship with Mason?"

"No, he never shared his feelings with me about anybody who came into the office or who he had dealings with. But I got so that I could read him and his attitudes pretty well."

"Others who came in?" I prompted.

"All three of those advisory board people would drop by, always separately and never even once as a group. I didn't much care for any of them if you are asking my opinion—or even if you aren't. I felt that Richmond woman was after Arthur, and I mean *really* after him. It was so obvious as to be a parody. I don't know where she learned to flirt, if that's what I can even call it, but her approach was somewhere between comical and just plain pathetic. And anyone could have seen that he wasn't interested in her, at least not in that way."

"Do you think she was husband hunting?"

"Huh! Well, I suppose that is a strong possibility, but she certainly didn't have the faintest idea of how to go about it. Sometimes, I had to keep from laughing. But Arthur either didn't notice or he ignored the woman's advances. He always seemed more or less friendly to her when I was present—in a business-like way, that is."

"How did Wordell relate to Sterling and Banks?"

"He seemed to tolerate them both, as much as he ever was civil to anyone; after all, he had handpicked them, along with the Richmond woman, to advise him. Sterling, now there was one cool customer, very much the old-school gentleman, although I always felt it was something of an act, just a little too slick for my taste."

"Was he trying too hard to play that 'old school' role?"

"I suppose you could say that. Now he was always very polite to me, very much the proper gentleman, so I have no complaints there. But I have always been good at seeing through people, and I didn't trust his apparent sincerity."

"What about the third member of that board?"

"That's Banks, Henry Banks, a squat, well-fed sort who seemed cheerful, although sometimes he overdid that sunshine and happiness act. It seemed like he was always telling Arthur what he thought he wanted him to hear. He could write a book about flattery. But he had an edge on him, and beneath that sunny exterior was a man that I could tell had pent-up anger."

"Didn't his fawning get on Wordell's nerves?"

"I think it did, but Arthur tried—not always successfully—to keep on good terms with the board members, since they had been brought in because he had lost confidence in Mason."

"I guess he felt he had to trust somebody," I observed.

She nodded, tight-lipped. "Then there was another visitor who came up to the twentieth floor quite a few times, named Boyd Tatum."

"The New York University professor."

"And he never let anyone forget it. He smoked a pipe, wore wool ties and tweed or corduroy jackets that had those patches on the elbows, and shoes that were scuffed. Oh, he seemed like a decent sort overall, very much like someone's favorite uncle, although of course that could have been an act. I heard him tell Arthur once that he appeared in amateur theatrical productions at the school.

"In any case, like everybody else who stopped in, he wanted to find favor with Arthur. In his case, the goal was clearly mercenary. In addition to teaching, he wrote biographies, and he badly wanted to do one on Arthur and his collection. He practically groveled in Arthur's presence."

"How did Wordell feel about that?"

"It was clear to me that he didn't like it. When Tatum came to the office on days I was working, their conversations seemed fairly civil, though. Arthur had dictated a couple of letters to Tatum telling him that he was mulling over the biography idea. He never said so, but it seemed to me that he was stalling the professor and didn't like him much, because when he was dictating the letters to him, he wore an even larger scowl than usual. And then, Arthur wrote a final letter to the man, telling him that under no circumstances would he cooperate in a biography."

"Why do you think he did that?"

"I'll tell you why. Arthur was simply not an attention seeker, rather the opposite. He avoided the spotlight and never sought publicity for himself."

"I saw an example of that at a dinner recently," I told her, recounting the episode where Wordell almost stormed out of the Waldorf ballroom in a huff.

"That sounds just like what I would have expected of him," Mabel said with conviction. "I am surprised that he really did not just get up and leave."

"I think he would have except for Nadia, who pleaded for him to stay. One other person I want to ask you about—Zondra Zagreb."

Her expression was telling, a scowl that needed no words, although that didn't stop her from supplying some choice ones. "That crazy artist whose appearance screams 'look at me, look at me!' What about her?"

"I gather that you have met."

"Only once, but that was enough, thank you. She stopped by to see Arthur one day."

"How did he react?"

"For some reason, he was happy to see the woman. She wanted to invite him to one of her showings, and he said that he would try to make it."

"Did he?"

"I really don't know," Mabel said. "I didn't keep Arthur's calendar, so I had little if any idea of what he did away from the office."

"I also have met Miss Zagreb, and she seemed somewhat impetuous."

"I would say immature, but then, I have had little experience with artists, and they live in a different world from mine. This one liked to tease Arthur, and he seemed to enjoy it!"

"Was she flirting with him, to use a word that came up with Miss Richmond?"

"I would rather not comment upon that. Arthur entrusted a great deal to me, and even though he is gone, I choose to honor his confidence."

"I gather you worked for Mr. Wordell only during the day."

"That is correct."

"Was he in the habit of visiting his Midtown office in the evenings?"

"Sometimes, yes. Arthur told me that he often liked to sit on his sill and look at his corner of the city at night. But he never, not once, asked me to work there after dark, which was just fine with me."

"Do you happen to know whether any of his visitors knew about these nocturnal visits of his?"

"I know why you're asking of course, and I wish I could tell you the answer, but I can't. I never knew myself if he had nighttime meetings up there. I have always assumed that he was alone when he wasn't dictating to me, but I have absolutely no way of knowing that."

"Did you ever have occasion to meet Wordell's wife?"

"No—and I must say I am very glad of it!"

"So we should not invite the two of you to the same party?"

"That is not in the least funny, Mr. Goodwin," she said, giving me a look that I could only describe as a glare.

"Sorry, my sense of humor is not for everyone; in fact, maybe it's not for anyone. Ignore my last statement. What is it about Mrs. Wordell that you don't like?"

"Just about everything. One of my most unpleasant tasks working for Arthur was having to write to that woman. She was always demanding more money, even beyond what I felt were the generous agreements that had been settled on. And then, she started trying to get her hands on some of Arthur's artwork."

"I gather he did not give in."

"Never! Although it was no business of mine, I thought that he had been more than fair to her in their settlement based on what I knew, and he was adamant about holding on to his art," Mabel Courtney said.

"And by the way, I happen to know that that woman also was loaded from all that money she got from her millionaire first husband. She was one of those people who don't ever seem to have enough. She always kept the pressure on Arthur with her demands for more."

"Why didn't she and Wordell get divorced?"

"I don't know, and I certainly was not about to ask him. Our relationship did not extend to personal questions, either from me or from him, which is the way it should be in business situations like ours."

"You have been very generous with your time, and you have been most helpful," I told Mabel as I rose to leave.

"Well, I am not so sure I would call anything I've said helpful, but at least I did not mince words, never have, never will."

"Do you have any plans now?"

"Do you mean, will I try to find a job? The answer is no, absolutely not. I really did not need the generous money that

Arthur paid me, although I took it because I earned it. I worked in a bunch of different jobs at the telephone company for more than thirty years and got a very comfortable pension. But I answered Arthur's advertisement and went to work for him because I found him interesting and plainspoken. I like plainspoken people, Mr. Goodwin."

"So do I; it saves beating around the bush. Again, thank you for your time, Miss Courtney."

She nodded grimly and held the door for me. I had been dismissed.

CHAPTER 9

I got back to the brownstone a few minutes after eleven, which meant Wolfe had come down from the plant rooms. As I walked into the office, he was going through the mail Fritz had stacked on his desk in my absence. "Miss Wordell called twice," he said, "and apparently she was upset."

"What do you mean, 'apparently'? Couldn't you tell?"

"Fritz took both calls, and now he is upset as well. It is not good for him to be out of sorts during the preparation of a meal."

I stared at Wolfe in wonder and almost asked why he didn't pick up the damned receiver himself, but I stopped myself. Why waste my breath? He didn't feel that he was placed on earth to answer squawking telephones.

Nadia Wordell's name and number were on a sheet on my desk blotter, printed neatly by Fritz. I picked up the phone and dialed.

"Oh, Mr. . . . Archie, are you all right?" she asked after I had identified myself.

"Never better. And why wouldn't I be?"

"I received a call earlier from the building where Daddy's office had been. The man said there had been a fight in that office and demanded to know who had been allowed to go in. I told them that it was none of their business as the space is still leased to us. He said that whoever it was who got into the office had started a brawl with one of their people."

"There is little if any truth to that report," I told her. "First, it was hardly a brawl unless one punch constitutes a brawl; second, the so-called brawl was initiated by a man who is in the building's employ and who acted like your office space was his personal domain. I don't believe he was badly hurt, probably just embarrassed by what happened to him."

"And you are all right?"

"I am. Would you like your key returned?"

"I really see no need for it," Nadia replied, and we said good-bye.

I hung up and turned toward Wolfe, who was glowering at me. "Well?" he demanded.

"Well, what?"

"Confound it, report!"

I did, giving him my morning's activities, beginning with the visit to Nadia and ending with my encounter with the man I choose to refer to as the moose.

"Was it necessary for you to resort to violence?" Wolfe asked after taking a drink of beer.

"I was not the one who resorted to violence, I merely retaliated when I got attacked. If I hadn't popped him one in the gut, we might still be fighting, beating each other silly. What I did was merciful, and it brought an end to the . . . hostilities. In the past when I have come home with a shiner or some bruises, you have found the sight repulsive. Look at my mug now: not a scratch on it."

"Pah! We are having a mushroom and almond omelet for lunch."

That was vintage Wolfe. On those rare occasions when I get in the last word during a discussion, he shifts to the subject of food.

Back in the office after eating, I turned to Wolfe. "Well, do we take Miss Wordell's case or not? We really shouldn't keep her dangling."

"What do you think?" That was another of Wolfe's tricks: making me decide whether we accept a client or not. The advantage for him is that if we do jump in and things go awry, I get the blame.

"I think we—" The telephone interrupted me. It was Lon Cohen of the *Gazette*. "Are you still interested in Arthur Wordell's death?" he asked as Wolfe picked up his receiver on my prompt.

"No comment," I said.

"Playing coy, eh? Well, so be it. I thought you and your boss might be interested in a story we'll be running in our final edition this afternoon. It seems the widow, the formidable Alexis Evans Farrell Wordell, is demanding a healthy portion of her late husband's art."

"This is Nero Wolfe, Mr. Cohen. Is the woman likely to be successful in her endeavor?"

"Too close to call, as our sportswriters like to say when they're handicapping a game. Our legal affairs reporter thinks she may have at least a chance, given that Wordell, for reasons known only to him, apparently died intestate and that the two of them never got divorced."

"Has Mrs. Wordell indicated what she would do with the art should she become its owner?"

"That is the sixty-four-dollar question, of course. The new Guggenheim wants the Wordell collection so badly they're salivating, and it's unclear as to what the widow's plans are. There is something else . . ."

"Yes, Mr. Cohen."

"Now understand, this is in the realm of hearsay, which we do not deal with in the pages of the *Gazette*. But you ought to know that something is making the rounds in *the whispering city*, as we call unconfirmed information."

"What is this 'something'?"

"That Nadia Wordell pushed her father to his death."

"An unlikely scenario. Do you have any idea how this originated?"

"No, rumors like that are almost always impossible to trace. Three of our reporters have gotten this from tipsters, who, granted, are not the most reliable of sources. But I thought you should be aware of what's being said. We don't plan to do anything about it, and I'll be surprised if a word of this pops up in any of the other dailies, even the tabloids."

"Thank you, Mr. Cohen," Wolfe said, cradling his receiver and turning to me as I also hung up.

"Do you have a comment?"

Long ago, Wolfe got it in his head that I am an expert on women, their moods, their foibles, their behavior. As much as I've tried to discourage his reliance on me in this area, he persists in casting me as an expert on the activities of the female gender.

"I suppose you want me to give you odds," I said.

"I do."

"Five to one against. That young woman would be no more likely to push her father off his windowsill perch than I would be to climb Mount Everest. As far as who might have started this rumor, I haven't got a clue."

Wolfe scowled and reached for his beer when the phone rang again, and once more it was Lon Cohen.

"This is getting to be a habit," I told him, silently mouthing his name to Wolfe, who got on the line.

"Just don't shoot the messenger, but I knew you were not likely to be reading today's issue of the *Mail & Express*, which just hit my desk," Lon said, referring to the city's raciest tabloid. "You two probably don't even know that its most-read column is the Keyhole Peeper."

"I can't and won't speak for my boss, but I have never read that feature and only heard it referred to offhand once or twice. In fact, I have also never read the *Mail & Express*."

"Well, you both are mentioned in the column today. Here is the item: 'Word is that rotund master sleuth Nero Wolfe and his two-fisted henchman, Archie Goodwin, are digging into the death of millionaire art collector Arthur Wordell, who fell twenty floors from a Midtown office window, and they are seeking a client. Could it be that murder is in the air?' "

"Where the hell did they dredge that up?" I said.

"These people have sources everywhere. For instance, have you talked to anyone about Wordell's death?"

"I plead the Fifth Amendment," I said.

"Oh, so that's the way it is?" Lon said. "If, by chance, any of the people connected with that sad event had occasion to visit you, it is just possible they were seen by the writer of the Keyhole Peeper, who seems to have more eyes than Argus. Your precious brownstone could be under surveillance by their sources, and maybe the building Wordell fell from, as well."

"Do people take this piffle seriously?" Wolfe asked.

"Sorry to say, some do. The column redefines irresponsible journalism, and it shoots from the hip, as if daring contradiction. Most people mentioned in its broadsides tend to ignore it and do not respond, often on the advice of an attorney. The question here is: Should the *Gazette* be ignoring it?"

"Mr. Cohen, we have had a long and mutually profitable relationship, and I would like it to continue. I believe you concur."

"I do."

"You have my word of honor, sir, that I have not yet accepted a commission to investigate the death of Mr. Wordell, although the subject has been discussed."

"Will you let us know if and when you do get a client?" Lon asked.

"I can promise nothing at this time, but I assure you the *Gazette* will be the first we communicate with if we have news we deem significant."

"That's the best I can ask for. Based on past experience, you should be prepared for an onslaught of telephone calls and doorbell ringing. Almost nobody admits to reading the Peeper, and even fewer say they take its items seriously. But as reckless and careless as the column is, we are well aware that it has impact. The career of a famous Hollywood actress was almost ruined by an item that claimed—falsely, as it turned out—that she was having an affair with a Mafia kingpin. It took her a long time to repair her image. Others have had similar experiences."

"Thank you for the warning, Mr. Cohen," Wolfe said, hanging up.

"Yeah, thanks a heap," I told Lon.

"As I said before, don't shoot the messenger. Besides, you're an old pro at stonewalling people. I should know."

"How you talk! I am the most cooperative of men."

"Right. I predict that your sense of cooperation is soon to be tested. If I were you, I'd take the phone off the hook for the next several days."

CHAPTER 10

There were times over "the next several days" Lon referred to when I wished I had heeded his advice and taken the damned telephone off the hook. The calls started coming not long after our conversation—from newspapers, television and radio stations, and, of course, Inspector Lionel T. Cramer of the New York Police Department's Homicide Squad.

First the press: I fielded calls from six daily papers—the *Times, Daily News, Journal-American, World-Telegram, Post*, and *Herald Tribune*. The dialogue was consistent: The caller, usually a beat reporter, started by asking if Nero Wolfe was investigating Arthur Wordell's death. My response: "What makes you think Mr. Wolfe has any interest in this man's demise?"

Then the fun began. None of the newshounds wanted to tell me they were following up on an item in (shudder) the Keyhole Peeper. I got answers like, "well, we've heard from our sources that . . ." and "there has been a lot of talk around town about . . ."

I remained businesslike and told each one of the callers that, "I am so sorry, but Nero Wolfe is not available for comment at this time." I hung up while each of them was still yammering. One reporter, a feisty, long-limbed, and intense fellow from the *Post*, rang our front doorbell and demanded to talk to Wolfe. I told him I was sorry but he never saw anyone without an appointment.

"Then how do I get an appointment?" the *Post* reporter demanded in frustration.

"You don't, because he only accepts appointments after a written request is submitted to me, by registered or certified mail. But don't hold your breath. I normally ignore registered and certified mail." I then closed the door and pretended not to hear the bell, which he leaned on until he gave up.

If you think I was having fun with these people, you are dead wrong. I was protecting Wolfe as well as trying to get my own work done in the office, which included a pile of his correspondence, unpaid bills, and orchid germination records that needed to be entered on file cards.

The television and radio folks were easier to discourage, being generally more polite and respectful and less aggressive than their print brethren. When I hung up on them, there was no yammering. And when a TV station film crew came to the door, I did what comes naturally—ignored the doorbell, which became silent after three rings.

Inspector Cramer was harder to ignore. Knowing the brownstone's schedule as well as I do, he came calling at a dozen minutes after eleven, which meant Wolfe was down from the morning visit with his concubines, as he referred to the ten thousand orchids he and the orchid nurse, Theodore Horstmann, so faithfully tended.

"Should I let him in?" I asked after seeing the thickset figure through the one-way glass in the front door.

"Confound it, yes!" Wolfe grumped. "We might as well see him and be done with it."

"We haven't had the pleasure of a visit from you for some time," I told the inspector after I pulled the door open and grinned.

"I don't know about you and Wolfe, but I haven't missed being here," Cramer muttered as he stepped inside, lumbered by me, and made a beeline for the office. By the time I caught up, he was planting himself in the red leather chair, which he had occupied more often than any other visitor to our abode.

"So . . . you figure Wordell got himself killed?" the inspector said, jabbing an unlit cigar in Wolfe's direction. "Trying to drum up business, is that the plan?"

"I find myself at a loss as to how to respond, sir."

"You, at a loss, hah! Now that's hard to believe. Just who is paying you?"

"I have no client," Wolfe said, spreading his hands, palms down, on the desk.

"That is not what I'm hearing."

"I would be most interested in the identity of your source."

"Don't give me that runaround. It's all over town."

"Indeed. And precisely what is it you are hearing?'

"I feel like I'm playing some sort of kids' game. Are you denying that you have been hired to find the so-called murderer of Arthur Wordell?" Cramer said, his face growing red.

"If a denial is even called for, then, yes."

"Balls! Are you saying that you have no client?"

"I am."

"Then why all the stuff that's going around?"

"I do not have an answer to that, sir, as I have no control over what is written or said about me. Now a question for you: Do you entertain doubt that Mr. Wordell was murdered?"

"Damn right I entertain it. He was a rich old eccentric who, for his own strange reasons, liked to amuse himself by sitting on a window ledge more than two hundred feet above the ground with his legs dangling on the outside. He lost his balance and fell, it's as simple as that. Hardly surprising for a man of his age.

"But don't think we did not at least consider that he might have been helped out of that window," the inspector continued. "The body was gone over for fabric or flakes of skin or hairs under the fingernails, for instance, on the off chance Wordell might have grabbed at an assailant, but there was nothing. Just why do you think that this was a killing?"

"I have not said I believe Mr. Wordell was murdered, but I understand there are those who feel his death was not an accident."

"Yeah, who, for instance?"

"Really, Mr. Cramer, are you telling me that no one has asked your department to investigate the gentleman's demise?"

"Okay, so both his widow and his daughter say that they think he was pushed off that ledge. And now it's even being said that the daughter was the one doing the pushing."

"Are you investigating the young woman?"

"Nah, that's just some rumor floating around," Cramer said, waving it away with a hand. "There's nothing to it."

"Perhaps similar to the rumor that I am investigating Mr. Wordell's death."

"That's different."

"Oh, and how is it different?"

"With the Wordell daughter, there has only been talk, but in your case, it has been in print."

"Where, may I ask?"

Cramer fidgeted, then cleared his throat and gave his necktie knot a tug. "In the . . . *Mail & Express*."

"Oh, yes . . . I believe I have heard of that publication. Don't they have a somewhat scurrilous column titled the Keyhole Peeper?"

"Uh, yeah."

"Did it happen to be in that column that my name appeared?"

Cramer nodded slowly, and, it seemed to me, with reluctance.

"Inspector, would you consider gossip to be a valuable and trustworthy source of information?"

"Aw, nuts!" he said, getting to his feet, his face flushed. "I knew it was a mistake coming over here. Don't bother getting up, Goodwin, I hate to see you strain yourself. I happen to know the way out."

"I guess you told him," I said to Wolfe when I returned to the office after double-locking the front door behind the inspector.

"Many people tend to believe everything that appears on a printed page, no matter how questionable the vehicle or how outrageous the statement. I am surprised to learn that Mr. Cramer appears to be one of those individuals," Wolfe said.

"*If it's in the paper, it must be true.* I've lost count of the number of times I've heard that," I added. "There are plenty of honest and hardworking journalists in town such as our own Lon Cohen, but like you I am surprised at Cramer, especially his buying something that ran in that Keyhole column."

Wolfe made a face and finished the first of the two beers Fritz had brought in. He turned to the morning mail when the phone rang.

"Nero Wolfe's office, Archie Goodwin speaking."

"I would like to speak to Mr. Wolfe. This is Frank Lloyd Wright." I covered my mouthpiece and quietly spoke the caller's name to Wolfe, who frowned and picked up his receiver.

"This is Nero Wolfe, Mr. Wright."

"I assume that you have heard of me."

"I have." If the architect expected Wolfe to sound impressed, he must have been disappointed. After several seconds of silence, Wright spoke. "I would like to have a meeting with you," he said.

"For what purpose, sir?"

"To discuss the death of Arthur Wordell."

"Do you possess information you wish to share?"

"Oh, no, no. But I think it is vital that the cause of Mr. Wordell's death be ascertained so that his wonderful collection of art finds its proper place—which is the Guggenheim Museum, of course. And I understand that you are working toward that end."

"That is not correct. I have no commission at this time."

"I still would like to meet with you," Wright said.

"I never leave home on business. Any conference would have to be held in my office."

I heard a huff on the other end of the line. "And just where is your office?"

Wolfe gave him our address. "I am available at nine tonight," he said.

Another huff. "It is not terribly convenient, but I will be there."

After everyone had hung up, I turned to Wolfe. "I'm surprised that you agreed to see him."

"It may prove instructive," he said. "I am sure we both will be able to endure it."

The doorbell rang at precisely nine that evening, one point in the famous architect's favor. I swung open the front door and found myself facing a man a couple of inches shorter than me wearing a black cape and a wide-brimmed porkpie hat. His face was lined—I knew him to be over ninety—but his expression showed the intensity of someone much younger. His light brown eyes studied me as if passing judgment. I held his gaze, unblinking.

"My name is Frank Lloyd Wright," he intoned, spacing the words as if expecting a reaction, which he did not get. "I am here to see Mr. Nero Wolfe. I have an appointment." He whipped off his cape and thrust it at me. I wanted to tell him to go to hell, but knowing my role, I took the coat and also his hat, hanging them on the rack and directing him down the hall to the office.

"An interesting room," Wright said, looking around as he planted himself in the red leather chair. "I could do wonders with it."

"Indeed, sir, and what wonders would those be?" Nero Wolfe asked as he entered the room and eased into the reinforced chair behind his desk.

"Where to start?" the architect said with a dismissive gesture.

"I happen to like this space precisely as it is," Wolfe stated. "Would you care for something to drink? I am having beer."

"Nothing for me. I came here to talk, not to imbibe."

"You requested this appointment, sir," Wolfe said as he pushed the buzzer that alerted Fritz to bring him his usual two bottles of Remmers. "Mr. Goodwin and I are known to be good listeners."

Wright cleared his throat. "I know that you both must be aware that I have created a museum structure here in Manhattan that is unlike any other, and I of course have a vested interest in seeing that it succeeds as an institution."

Wolfe popped the cap off one of the bottles that had been set before him, never taking his eyes from his guest. "I have read about your museum and have seen photographs and renderings of it in the newspapers."

"Then I am sure you must agree that the Guggenheim will be a marvelous asset to New York, a city in which I know that you have lived for many years and are a well-respected resident."

"As to the museum being an asset, I claim no expertise either in art or in architecture, so I leave it to others to enumerate the merits of both the structure and its contents," Wolfe replied.

"Do you know anything at all about me?" our visitor asked, tilting his head to one side.

"I am aware you were born Frank Lincoln Wright in Wisconsin soon after the end of the Civil War, but that you changed your middle name to honor your mother's family, the Lloyd Joneses. I know that in the previous century, you started your career in the office of the eminent designer Louis Sullivan, whom you referred to as your *lieber meister*. I know you developed what you term as 'organic architecture,' and I am aware you designed a home that is constructed over a waterfall in Pennsylvania, as well as many other residences, the largest number in Illinois, and a hotel in Tokyo that is said to have withstood an earthquake."

"The Imperial Hotel most definitely *did* withstand an earthquake, and that building survives to this day. I see that you have studied up on me," Wright said in a tone that showed he was clearly impressed.

"Not intentionally," Wolfe replied. "I happen to read a great deal, and I remember everything I read. In addition, of course, I have read articles about you recently that relate to this new museum."

Wright shifted in his chair and scowled. "As things stand, the death of Arthur Wordell may have thrown a monkey wrench into the future of the Guggenheim."

"How can that be?" Wolfe asked, spreading his hands, palms up. "As has been noted in the newspapers, Mr. Wordell's collection would be but one element among the many works planned for display in the new museum."

"But it is a very significant element," our guest said. "Without it, the Guggenheim would lose at least some of its luster. It is vitally important that the circumstances of Mr. Wordell's demise be cleared up."

"What does that have to do with me?"

"I understand you are investigating his death."

"Where did you read or hear that?"

"I cannot remember," the architect said.

"It is not true."

"Based on what I have come to know about you, that is indeed a pity."

"Are you proposing to hire me?

"Oh, no, no, not myself," Wright replied, casting the idea away with the wave of a hand. "I have learned that your fees are substantial, and I am certainly in no position to afford them. Whatever you may have heard about the money an architect earns, it is highly exaggerated, I assure you."

"Are you then suggesting a client other than yourself?"

"I am not. As I said earlier, you are a longtime and well-regarded resident of this city, and I would think you might see it as a civic duty to investigate Arthur Wordell's death and in the process clear the way for his art to become a vital element in the Guggenheim collection."

Wolfe drained the beer from his glass and popped open the second bottle. "Sir, my civic duty, to use your words, is to pay my taxes and to conduct myself in a lawful and orderly manner. I have no other responsibilities, either to the municipality or to its millions of residents. You and I both sell our services, we do not give them away. I cannot imagine that you would design a building and not expect compensation."

Wright stiffened and made a face. "It seems clear to me that my visit has been fruitless, and there is no point in our continuing this conversation. I bid you a good evening." He rose, walking briskly out of the office and down the hall. I followed him to the front door and attempted to help him on with his cape, but he rebuffed the offer, slinging it over his shoulders and donning his porkpie hat with a flourish.

"And a good evening to you, too," I said to his back as he went down the steps to the curb. As I watched him climb into the backseat of a waiting prewar Lincoln Continental, I wondered if two such outsize egos had ever been in the same room before.

Back in the office, I slipped into my desk chair and turned to face Wolfe, who had picked up his latest book, *The Ugly American* by Lederer and Burdick. "Well, how does it feel to have been in the presence of the man who, without blushing, has been known to call himself 'the greatest architect in the world'?"

"Pfui. Mr. Wright may well possess talent in his field, but he also is a poseur. To suggest I would undertake what may well be a murder investigation without a client is preposterous. His visit has been futile, and were he possessed with a modicum of sense, he would not have undertaken it."

"Let me list you as unimpressed by Mr. Frank Lloyd Wright."

"List me in any way you choose, Archie, but do not make any future appointments with the man, not that I expect him to request them." I started to reply, but his face was hidden by the open book, a signal the discussion was at its end.

CHAPTER 11

We continued to get telephone calls from the press about the Wordell death, but over the next few days, they gradually decreased to the point that I figured everybody in the city of New York and its environs now realized that Nero Wolfe was not investigating the death of a noted art collector.

I thought I probably had heard the last of these calls on a blue-sky morning when I sat at my desk in the office with coffee and answered, as I always do during working hours, "Nero Wolfe's office, Archie Goodwin speaking."

"Mr. Goodwin, my name is Alexis Evans Farrell Wordell," she said, spacing her four names and giving each one of them equal emphasis. "You probably know who I am."

"I am afraid I do not," I replied, not wishing to make things easier for her. "What can we do for you?"

Her sniff of disapproval came through the line. "I would like to make an appointment to see Mr. Nero Wolfe."

"May I tell him the subject?"

"Really, Mr. Goodwin, should that not be obvious?"

"I regret to say that it is not to me."

The sniff was replaced with a drawn-out sigh. "I want to discuss the possibility of engaging Mr. Wolfe to investigate the death of my husband, Arthur Wordell. The police appear to be totally uninterested."

"I will inform Mr. Wolfe of your request and determine if or when he would be available to see you. Where can I reach you?"

More sighing, followed by a telephone number. "Are you able to give me some idea as to when I would get some response from Mr. Wolfe?" she asked.

"I will relay your request to him later this morning. I must tell you, however, that he is extremely busy."

"I know by reputation that Mr. Wolfe charges high fees, and I am prepared to discuss those fees with him."

"I will be sure to tell him that. Thank you for your call." I knew she wanted to press me further, but I did not give her the chance and hung up before she could ask more questions.

When Wolfe came down from the plant rooms at eleven and walked into the office, I said, "The world is beating a path to your door."

He settled in behind his desk and buzzed for beer without replying.

"Aren't you going to ask me about our latest caller?"

"I have a feeling you are going to tell me," he grumbled as he went through the morning mail.

"Try Alexis Evans Farrell Wordell on for size," I said. "You may remember that she—"

"I remember. What does the woman want?"

"To hire you to find her husband's—make that her estranged husband's—killer, of course."

"Did you tell her I am not investigating Mr. Wordell's death?"

"No, I thought that we might initiate a bidding war between her and Nadia Wordell. You know, get each of them to try topping the other for your services. It could turn out to be quite a contest."

"Twaddle!"

"No, sir, not twaddle. I know you feel our bank balance is at a comfortable level now, which happens to be true at the moment. But given the resources it takes to run this operation, you also are well aware of how quickly that almighty balance can be depleted."

"Archie, do you believe Mr. Wordell was pushed to his death?"

"I don't know."

"Nor do I. We could accept a commission from either of these women, but to what end? Would we be taking the money of one or the other of them under false pretenses?"

"I suppose that is possible. But both of them, and Frank Lloyd Wright as well, seem to think this was murder."

"That is demonstrably true only in Miss Wordell's case. The other two have surely been led to believe the veracity of the fabricated newspaper item that claimed I was investigating the Wordell death."

"So you don't plan to see the Wordell widow?"

"I did not say that, Archie. The daughter has not yet provided any evidence that her father was murdered, but the other Wordell woman may have some insights. See if she can be here at two thirty."

"That is somewhat short notice."

"She has requested the appointment, not I."

"Point taken. I will call the lady now." She answered immediately, and I told her what Wolfe had said.

"I have a luncheon today. Would he be able to see me at another time?"

"Mr. Wolfe has a very crowded calendar," I replied, not offering the imperious Mrs. Wordell an alternative.

After a pause of several seconds came her response. "All right, I will be there. I have the address," she said in tone that indicated she was not pleased.

Like F. L. Wright before her, the widow Wordell arrived promptly. I opened the door to her and took note of a black Bentley purring at the curb with a uniformed chauffeur behind the wheel. "Please come in," I said, and her thank-you was a thin smile, nothing more, not even a nod.

"You are Mr. Goodwin, of course."

"I am. Please come this way." I led her down the hall to the office and aimed her at the red leather chair, which she gracefully eased into. Alexis had to be at least sixty, although she could pass for a decade younger. Her well-coiffed dark hair had stylish streaks of gray, and her face was unlined. If that meant she had had work done, you will have to ask someone smarter than me. She was wearing a red Chanel suit that fit her beautifully, and lest you wonder if I am an expert on women's fashions, the answer is no; Lily Rowan owns a few Chanel creations, and she has pointed out to me some of the hallmarks of that designer.

Our guest looked at me questioningly, as if asking where Wolfe was. At that moment, he stepped into the room, detoured around the desk, and sat, dipping his chin slightly in Alexis's direction. "Madam."

"Mr. Wolfe," she said, unsmiling, "thank you for seeing me." If the woman was surprised at his dimensions or the fact that he did not offer to shake hands, she did not show it.

"Would you like refreshments? I am having beer."

"No, thank you."

"You believe your husband was murdered, is that correct?"

"You get right to the point, don't you?" she said, nodding. "I refuse to accept the idea that Arthur would have lost his balance and fallen from that ridiculous windowsill where he insisted on sitting on so many occasions."

"I understand you and he had not lived together for years."

"That is correct."

"Why did you separate?"

She stiffened. "I did not realize that I was going to be subjected to an interrogation here."

Wolfe looked at her with eyebrows raised. "Madam, I am an investigator. My raison d'être is to probe, to delve, to seek answers. Do you find my question to be of an offensive nature?"

"Oh, I suppose not," she said, exhaling. "Arthur and I had become . . . well, we had grown apart. When I married him, I did not realize how single-minded he was in his quest for great works of art. That lust for acquisitions is all that he seemed to live for. You might term it an obsession."

"But you did not divorce."

"We both had been married before, as you may know, and both our spouses had died. And I am a Roman Catholic, so neither I nor my church believe in divorce. Also, I felt that someday we might get back together."

"Was Mr. Wordell similarly inclined?"

"With Arthur, you could not always tell, strange as that may sound," she said. "He was hard to read. I told him that I felt we should try living apart for a while, and he had nothing to add, not a single word."

"Did he provide for you financially?"

"He was . . . always most generous."

"What about his estate?"

"He apparently has left no will."

"That seems highly unusual for an individual with the extent of Mr. Wordell's assets."

"One would think so," Alexis said. "But I am very suspicious."

"Of whom or what?"

"Of his daughter. Have you met her?"

"Briefly."

"Well, do not be fooled by her wide-eyed, little-girl innocence. She is far from what she seems."

"In what way, madam?"

"She is a conniver, and she may very well have pushed Arthur out of that window herself."

"Really? Do you possess any evidence to back up that suspicion?"

Alexis shifted in her chair and brushed an errant hair from her smooth forehead. "I do not," she said, "but I have a feeling, and there has been talk."

"What kind of talk?"

Alexis waved the question away. "One hears things," she replied in an ominous tone, rolling her eyes.

"What would cause the young woman to commit patricide?" Wolfe asked.

"I cannot answer for the actions of my stepdaughter. I find her to be an unbalanced individual."

"Let us for the moment stipulate that your husband was murdered, which I am not ready to concede, but no matter. What drives you to find his killer?"

"Why shouldn't I want the murderer found? Isn't that what a wife should do, even one who has been separated from her husband?"

"Do you expect to receive all or a portion of Mr. Wordell's art collection?"

"I find that question to be impertinent."

"Impertinent—why is that?"

"It seems to me that is none of your business."

Wolfe shrugged. "Perhaps. Have you spoken to the police?"

"I have, on two occasions. They did not seem interested in the least in my thoughts, and they refused to consider this a murder case. I happen to believe that they have taken that stance because it is just simpler for them to avoid having to conduct an investigation."

"If I may file a demurrer, madam, I have had occasion over the years to interact with this city's police department in numerous situations, and despite their limitations, I have never found them to shy away from a murder investigation merely because it would entail time and/or effort."

"Are you suggesting that Arthur's death was not murder?" Alexis asked.

"I am suggesting no such thing. But I would prefer to see stronger evidence that he was pushed to his death."

"I am afraid that I have nothing to offer you as proof other than my intense belief that he was murdered and my suspicion involving Arthur's daughter."

"I am unable to help you," Wolfe told her.

"You mean you will not accept my money to investigate Arthur's death?" she said. "I assure you that I am able to afford your rates. Name any amount you choose, and I will write a check now." She pulled a checkbook from her purse and laid it on the corner of his desk.

"I do not for one moment doubt your financial wherewithal, but I have yet to see any evidence of murder. Besides, if I decide to undertake an investigation, it may well be for someone who previously offered to engage me."

"And just who is that?"

"I am not at liberty to say."

"So—you got me to come here under false pretenses," Alexis snapped. "You were pumping me for information! I guess I should have expected as much from a private detective."

"Keep in mind that it was you who sought me out, madam, not the other way around. And I did not—"

Wolfe stopped talking because he had lost his audience. Alexis Evans Farrell Wordell stood, pivoted smartly, and walked out of the office without a word, head high. It was an exit worthy of a Broadway star or an opera diva.

I followed her down the hall and was impressed at the pace she set in her stiletto heels. She was out the door before I could hold it open for her, and I was left to shut and lock it behind her. She clicked down the front steps to the waiting Bentley still idling at the curb and never once looked back.

"Well, I guess she just made a statement," I said to Wolfe back in the office. He glared at me and returned to his current book.

CHAPTER 12

So three people had now come calling, asking Wolfe to investigate a death that might or might not be a murder, and two of them even offered to throw money at us. When my boss came down from the plant rooms at six, I waited until he had gotten seated and buzzed for beer, then turned to him.

"We really owe Miss Wordell some sort of response," I said. "If we are not going to look into her father's death, maybe we should recommend our old friend Del Bascomb or some other first-rate agency and not keep her hanging."

Before he could respond, the telephone rang. It was Lewis Hewitt.

"Hello, Mr. Goodwin," he said as I signaled Wolfe to pick up his receiver. "I am calling for my goddaughter, Nadia. She is wondering whether Mr. Wolfe has decided if he will take her on as a client, but she is afraid to bother him."

"I am on the line," Wolfe said. "I am glad for the chance to talk to you without Miss Wordell present or within earshot.

Such was not possible when you were here with her, and that inhibited our discussion. Do you agree with her that her father was murdered?"

"I have thought about this a lot the last few days. The more I have mulled it over, the more convinced I am that Arthur was pushed, and I can give you my thoughts as to why."

"Please do."

"First, Arthur was in extremely good shape. Just weeks ago, I had accompanied him to his annual physical examination, and his doctor pronounced him every bit as fit as a man twenty years younger than he.

"Second, he also was mentally keen—eccentric, without a doubt, but very sharp. He showed no signs whatever of what I would describe as senility. Third, he exhibited no indication of depression so that, as far as I am concerned, any suggestion of suicide is simply out of the question. He was enjoying life far too much.

"And fourth, the idea that he lost his balance and fell I feel is absolute nonsense! He had been doing that weird windowsill business of his for years. I had even seen him do it on one occasion, and although I thought it was a crazy stunt, he certainly seemed agile and self-possessed to me."

"When you were here with Miss Wordell, she was reluctant to suggest anyone who might want to harm her father. Do you share her reluctance?"

"Before I answer, I should point out that Nadia, as you probably were able to tell, is extremely reserved, maybe shy is a more accurate word. She essentially grew up without a mother, as Arthur's first wife died before the girl was even a teenager. And relatively late in life, he found himself trying to rear a daughter by himself, far from an easy task, even for a far younger man than Arthur."

"I gather Mr. Wordell's second wife was not cut out to be a stepmother," Wolfe said dryly.

Hewitt laughed. "That is an understatement. To her, Nadia was just someone who got in her way, or would have had she ever lived in the house with the two of them. But as you may know, she was away at boarding school or university most of the time they were married and living together. In all honesty, I can't begin to explain to you why Arthur married Alexis. She is a handsome woman, without doubt, but I never saw the mutual attraction. Have you met her?"

"I have. I gather you did not like her."

"Let me frame it this way," Hewitt said, clearing his throat. "Arthur and I continued to see each other after he remarried, but it was just the two of us, at dinner in a restaurant or at any number of clubs in Midtown that one or the other of us belongs to. During his first marriage, we and our wives would often get together for a meal or to see a play. Neither my wife nor I had any desire in being around Alexis, however, and she had no interest in being in our company, for that matter.

"Now, on to your question: At first, I tended to view Nadia's insistence that her father had been killed as a denial of his carelessness while on that damned windowsill. But the more I thought about it, the more I have come to believe she is right, especially given what I know about Arthur's physical and mental health, which I have just alluded to."

"Do you have any idea who wanted him dead?"

"I do not," Hewitt said. "He could be irascible, of course, and he did not care at all about what people thought of him, so he was hardly one for making friends. I was always puzzled as to why he seemed to like my company; maybe it was because I was nonthreatening, at least in those areas where he possessed expertise." The two men exchanged a few more words, and then the conversation ended.

Some words here on the relationship between Wolfe and Lewis Hewitt. They have been acquainted for years, drawn together by their mutual passion for orchids. They dine at each other's home about once a year, and sometimes they attend the Metropolitan Orchid Show together. Theirs is what I would term a friendly rivalry, with some envy tossed in when one of them possesses an exotic orchid the other covets, which is often. They never call each other by name, which always has seemed strange to me, but I have chalked it up to a kind of reserve that is observed by the generation older than mine.

After they ended their conversation, Wolfe sat for several minutes, eyes unblinking, staring across the room at . . . well, I have no idea what he was staring at. I had seen that look before on occasion. Based on the past, it indicated that he was about to make a decision.

Further mention of Lewis Hewitt is in order: Although he has never told me this and never will, Nero Wolfe has a healthy respect for Hewitt's opinions, and not just those involving the world of orchids. I have been present at enough of their dinners to know that when Hewitt speaks on any number of subjects, Wolfe listens and often agrees.

Hewitt seems to be convinced that Wordell had been helped out of that window perch of his, and although this is rarely the case, I felt I could predict what action Wolfe would now be taking. I did not have long to wait for my prediction to come true.

"Archie, telephone Mr. Cohen."

I dialed Lon at the *Gazette*, and he answered immediately, barking his last name, while Wolfe picked up his instrument.

"I know, I know, don't tell me," I said. "You happen to be juggling seven deadlines and haven't got time to take a deep breath, let alone talk, but put all that on hold for the moment, because someone needs to speak to you, and you really should listen to what he has to say."

"Mr. Cohen, this is Nero Wolfe. You will recall that during an earlier conversation, I told you that if we had any news for you about the Wordell demise that we deemed significant, we would inform you."

"I remember that quite clearly."

"I have decided to undertake an investigation into the death of Arthur Wordell."

"Really? Do you have a client?"

"I do."

"Will you tell me that individual's name?"

"No, sir."

"All right, I know that beggars can't be choosers. What has changed your mind and made you decide to take on the case?"

"My determination that any other explanation for Mr. Wordell's death is inexplicable."

"That's not very specific," Lon complained.

"That is all I am able to offer at the moment. Do you have enough to write a story?"

"Absolutely. This is too good to bury in one of our gossip columns, so we'll play it as a news story, probably at the top of page three. And we will be sure to point out that you made your decision today. The last thing we want is for the *Mail & Express* to claim that their blasted column, the Keyhole Peeper, had the story first. Every paper in town, including us, is sick of that columnist's boast that 'We report the news *before* it happens.' "

"Mr. Cohen, I assure you that I have not spoken to anyone from the Keyhole Peeper and I never will."

"I appreciate that and also appreciate the exclusive. The article will appear in all our editions tomorrow, including the one that will hit your doorstep late in the morning."

"Will it contain a photograph?"

"Of you? Of course. I know that we have your most recent head shot on file," Lon said. Wolfe likes to see his name—and his picture—in the newspaper as much as anyone. He claims that it is good for business, heaven forbid that vanity might have anything to do with it.

"Well, we need to be prepared for another onslaught of calls and an incessant ringing of our doorbell," I told Wolfe after we had hung up with Lon, "including the usual complaints from the other papers as to why you continue showing favoritism to the *Gazette*."

"Let the other newspapers carp until they are hoarse from their carping," Wolfe said.

"Easy for you to say," I told him, "as I am the one left to deal with all those angry people and institutions. But that's all right, I'm used to it and I believe it is written somewhere in my job description. May I assume that Nadia Wordell is now our client?"

"You may."

"Shouldn't we let her in on that fact? She may be surprised, especially if she happens to read the *Gazette*."

"Telephone Miss Wordell. Let her know of my decision and ask her to come here tomorrow afternoon at two thirty. If she desires that Mr. Hewitt accompany her, all well and good. In fact, I believe that is preferable."

"Your wish, et cetera," I said, picking up the phone and dialing Nadia. She was delighted with the news. "Will Mr. Wolfe then tell me what I am to owe him?" she asked.

"Oh, yes, you can be sure of that," I told her. "And please feel free to bring Mr. Hewitt along as well."

"I will and thank you! You may be aware that he has been almost like a second father to me."

"All right, she will be here with Hewitt tomorrow," I said to Wolfe. "Once the *Gazette* early edition hits the streets in the morning, do you want to take bets on who we will hear from first, Cramer, the widow Wordell, or any one of half a dozen newspapers?"

"I will pass on the wagering, but I would be surprised if we do not get either a call or, more likely, a visit, from the inspector."

CHAPTER 13

It was hardly a surprise that the next morning did indeed bring a visit from Homicide Inspector Cramer, who rang our bell at three minutes after eleven.

"The least you can do," I told our glowering visitor as I opened the front door to him, "is to delay your arrival until Mr. Wolfe gets himself settled in the office. He just came down from the plant rooms and barely has had time to put in an order for his beer."

"Well, dammit, I sure would not want to inconvenience him now, would I?" Cramer said as he strode down the hall to the office with me at his heels. He dropped himself into the red leather chair just as Wolfe was uncapping the first of two bottles of frosty Remmers that had been set before him.

"So that blasted column was right after all!" the inspector barked, sticking his chin out.

"I beg your pardon, sir," Wolfe responded, eyes wide in a look that feigned innocence.

"The last time I was here, which seems like only yesterday, you claimed that item in the Keyhole Peeper about you having a client on the so-called Wordell murder was false. Hah!"

"It was false, sir," Wolfe said evenly. "When you visited us, I did not have a client. I do now."

"This much I have learned from Stebbins, who got hold of a copy of the *Gazette*'s first edition. Okay, who hired you?"

"Come, come, Mr. Cramer. You know better than to ask that."

"Hell, I know better than to ask you anything; that is, if I want something that resembles a straight answer. You're saying you are positive that Wordell was helped off that windowsill?"

"I am."

"Care to share your thoughts with me? I'm a little slow on the draw, or so I've been told."

Wolfe drew in a gallon of air and let it out slowly. "First, despite his age, Mr. Wordell was by all accounts in excellent physical condition. Only weeks before his death, he underwent a physical examination and was found to be as fit as someone much younger than he. Second, those who knew him best said he showed no signs whatever of mental deterioration. Third, he had been perching on that Midtown windowsill for years without a mishap."

"That is not to say he finally tried that stunt once too often and slipped," Cramer insisted. "You can't deny that possibility. I have seen that sill myself, and it's awfully narrow."

"So Archie has said to me. However, the odds of his accidentally falling are so long as to be infinitesimal, as I see it."

Cramer, grim-faced, pursed his lips. "Well, I sure as hell can't stop you from believing what you choose to believe. And I know that you have to make money, plenty of it, to keep this joint of yours afloat," he said with a sweeping gesture of his extended arm as if to encompass the entire brownstone. "I will be on my way," he said, getting to his feet.

After the inspector had left and I had locked the door behind him, I turned to Wolfe. "You know darned well why he's so depressed right now. He is aware that when the commissioner reads about your investigation, he will demand that Cramer start considering Wordell's death as a murder."

"I cannot be responsible for the actions of the police department's commissioner or the burdens those actions may place upon Mr. Cramer," Wolfe said. "Furthermore—yes, what is it?"

Fritz Brenner had come in, and he was clutching several sheets of paper. During Cramer's visit, I had shut off both office phones, so Fritz had been tasked with being our answering service, a not uncommon practice in the brownstone.

"Several calls came in," he said, handing me the sheets, "including one from an angry and unpleasant woman." He went back to the kitchen, clearly upset that his preparation of rice fritters with black currant jam and endive salad with tarragon had been delayed by all the telephone traffic.

"Let us see," I said, paging through Fritz's neatly printed notes. "Ah, yes, here is our angry woman, in Fritz's words: 'Mrs. Wordell telephoned and was most upset. She heard that Mr. Wolfe has taken on a client and she called him a *traitor*—that is the word she used—and then she said a few more things that I refuse to repeat and hung up. It was most distressing.'

"According to Fritz's notes, we also got calls from the *Times*, *Daily News*, and *Herald Tribune*. That's a lot of calls in a short time. It would seem that everybody wants to talk to you." Wolfe drank beer and remained silent.

"Wait, I am not done yet. Lon will be delighted to learn how many people read the *Gazette*'s early edition. Others who phoned and want an audience with you are Boyd Tatum and Zondra Zagreb—I know you recognize their names. Each of them seems willing to come here."

"Anything else?"

"No, sir. As I said, that's a bunch of calls Fritz had to answer one after the other, which hasn't improved his disposition. And it figures that plenty more will be coming."

"We will see Mr. Tatum and . . . Miss Zagreb," Wolfe said, sighing before he pronounced the latter name.

"When would you like them here? Together, or separately?"

"Separately. Inquire as to whether Mr. Tatum can be present tonight at nine. If so, call the woman and suggest tomorrow night at the same time."

The doorbell rang just before two thirty. I admitted Nadia Wordell and Lewis Hewitt, both of whom greeted me with nods and friendly but tight smiles. In the office, I steered Nadia to the red leather chair while Hewitt took a yellow one.

Wolfe started to speak, but our new client jumped in first, pulling a checkbook from her purse and setting it on Wolfe's desk, much as Alexis had done not long before. "I am so glad you are taking me as a client, Mr. Wolfe," she said. "I will pay whatever figure you wish."

"That can wait," Wolfe told her, holding up a palm. "When you were here previously, I was dissatisfied with your responses to my questions."

Nadia's narrow shoulders sagged, and her face assumed a downcast expression. "I am . . . so sorry. Of course, I want to be of whatever help I can."

"And she means that," Hewitt put in, playing the role of godfather.

"Very well," Wolfe addressed Nadia. "You seem positive in your assertion your father was killed. Yet on your earlier visit, you declined to suggest any possible malefactor. That is an unsat-isfactory response, Miss Wordell. If I am to pursue this investiga-tion effectively, I will need more cooperation than I previously received from you." Nadia swallowed hard and nodded.

"Now, let us start again. Which of your father's acquain-tances had the most to gain from his death?"

"I really can't think of a single one of them who stood to profit from . . . well, from what happened."

"Did you sense any animosity toward him from any of his associates, or anyone else who had dealings with him?"

"No one I can think of."

"Very well," Wolfe said, keeping his irritation in check. "Let us approach this from another direction. Who among your father's circle, and make that circle as wide as you choose, was he antagonistic toward?"

Nadia closed her eyes as if in thought, which I hoped was the case. "Daddy never really cared very much for Roger Mason," she said. "He told me Roger was morose and a stuffed shirt—I remember clearly that was the phrase he used, 'a stuffed shirt.' "

"Yet he had appointed Mr. Mason to be the curator of his collection."

"That is true, but after a couple of years or so, he put together that three-person advisory group because he seemed unhappy with Roger's leadership."

"What did your father see as Mr. Mason's shortcomings?"

"Daddy never got specific, at least not to me, other than to mention Roger's less-than-winning personality and his overall sour attitude."

"Can you conceive of Mr. Mason pushing your father to his death?"

She shook her head and wrinkled her brow. "That is hard for me to believe, Mr. Wolfe. I'm afraid that I don't possess the knowledge that Hamlet did. His father's ghost told him who his murderer was."

"It is true, you do not have the advantage of having experienced a specter, but you were the closest person to your father, were you not?"

"I like to think so. I cannot imagine anyone who would have been any closer."

"Very well, then let us continue. Setting Mr. Mason aside for now, did your father make disparaging remarks about any other individuals who might be considered as suspects?"

When Nadia hesitated, Wolfe prompted. "We will begin with Mr. Sterling."

"Emory? He has always been my idea of the perfect gentleman—well dressed, well mannered, elegant, and very kind, with manners that few people seem to possess anymore. I remember that when Daddy decided to assemble that advisory group, Emory was the first one he thought of. He had great respect both for the man and for his publication, which he had subscribed to for a long time."

"Did the magazine—*Art & Artists*, I believe—ever do an article about your father or his collection?"

"They had planned to, two or three years ago it was."

"What did Mr. Wordell think about the feature?"

"It was the one time I ever saw Daddy have a strong disagreement with Emory. I remember that Emory showed the piece to Daddy in advance, and he felt it was far too much about himself and not enough about the collection. They argued, and finally Emory very reluctantly agreed to kill the article, which was to have been the next issue's cover story. I don't think the two of them were ever as close after that episode, even though Daddy did appoint Emory to his advisory board."

"I would like to move on to Henry Banks. How would you describe his relationship with your father?"

"It was my impression that he irritated Daddy sometimes. He seemed to be the type who wanted to please everybody, at least superficially but that demeanor has always appeared to be somewhat forced to me, as if he was trying too hard. Maybe that comes from his having to curry favor with those whose collections he curated. I always felt he had a suppressed anger just beneath the surface, although I really couldn't tell you why. On the surface, his behavior was like what you might expect from a salesman—always upbeat and optimistic."

"And ready to whip out his order book," I put in.

"Exactly!" Nadia said, clapping once and breaking into the first smile since she had arrived.

"Had your father any substantive reason to resent or dislike Mr. Banks?" Wolfe asked.

"I really don't believe so. What do you think?" she said, turning and addressing Hewitt.

He nodded to his goddaughter. "You have pretty well summarized the man, from what I have seen of Mr. Banks, although I cannot claim to know him well. As you have said, he seemed to be trying, sometimes too hard, to be everybody's friend. I would use the word *ingratiating* to describe him."

"What about Miss Richmond?" Wolfe posed.

"Oh, I think Daddy liked her well enough, but only in small doses," Nadia said. "Those big glasses distracted him because they made her eyes look so big. Now there is no question she is smart—as are all these people we have been talking about. But Faith—Miss Richmond—could be intense in discussing art, and that intensity sometimes made Daddy feel that he was being lectured to, which he did not appreciate one bit."

"Nevertheless, he hired the woman to be on his advisory board."

"Absolutely. As he once told me, it was not necessary to like a person to respect their abilities."

"An eminently defensible position," Wolfe said. "Tell us your thoughts about Mr. Tatum."

"Boyd? I overheard somebody at a party once—I can't remember who now—describe him as the quintessential Ivy League professor, even though NYU is not an Ivy League school," Nadia said, "and I would agree with that. He's pleasant to be around, full of anecdotes about artists and the art world, and maybe a little on the gossipy side, but never in a mean or a caustic way, at least from what I've seen. I was always under the impression that Daddy liked him, at least early in their relationship, although Boyd could be quite insistent, particularly when it came to his desire to do that biography."

"Of your father?"

"Oh, yes, I'm sorry, I thought I had mentioned that earlier. Boyd has done several biographies of both artists and collectors—some of them full-length books, others extensive articles in scholarly journals and in university publications. People have told me that his work is well thought of."

"How did Mr. Wordell feel about this project?" Wolfe asked.

"He seemed to resist the idea. Daddy had an ego, there is no question about it, but overall, he liked to stay out of the limelight. I think that being a center of attention embarrassed him and made him uneasy."

"I sure got an excellent illustration of that at the Waldorf dinner when that ingratiating master of ceremonies tried to get your father to stand up and be recognized," I said.

"Yes, that is a perfect example," Nadia said, tossing a smile in my direction. "On other occasions, he refused to be interviewed when newspaper or television reporters called.

" 'I don't want any publicity,' he would grumble. 'Everything I do, everything I buy, speaks for itself and needs no explanation.' "

"Straightforward and understandable," Wolfe remarked.

"Daddy was nothing if not straightforward," his daughter replied. "He never liked to play games with people. Everyone always knew just where they stood with him, although they did not always like the fact that he could be terribly blunt to the point of being insulting."

"Back to Mr. Tatum. Did your father ever tell him definitely that he did not want to be the subject of a biography?"

"That I really can't say for sure, Mr. Wolfe, although the subject may have caused some friction between the two men. I think you would have to ask Boyd that yourself. However, knowing Daddy, I find it hard to believe he would have wanted to be written about."

"Tell me about Zondra Zagreb."

Nadia laughed, which was a welcome sound. "Oh my, just where should I begin? Now Zondra, she is a true original—calculating in the image she has created, to be sure. But those who know their art far better than I do tell me that she also is immensely talented in her particular genre, which is abstract expressionism. In fact, if I were her, I would definitely tone down her personal flamboyance. I believe that it sometimes gets in the way of people taking her art seriously."

"Is the woman possessed of a temper?"

"She can flare up, there is no question of that. I heard about an incident at one of her showings a while back where some man sniggered about one of her pieces, demeaning it to his friends. She lashed out at him and used words that you would not be likely to hear in a Manhattan art gallery. Someone who was there thought she was actually going to hit the man, but of course she didn't."

"Did your father appreciate her artistic talents?"

"I think based on what little he told me, he was of two minds about Zondra's work. He felt she was technically skilled, but he really wasn't drawn to abstract art as much as to other genres, so he had a hard time identifying with or appreciating her canvases."

"I have yet to meet Miss Zagreb, but Archie tells me she is a woman of some substance," Wolfe said.

Nadia knew that he was referring to Zondra's physique and, after a glance at the far larger specimen facing her, she nodded. "Yes . . . Zondra is definitely good-sized, although she carries herself well. Part of me envies her flair."

"So, physically, she would be capable of pushing your father from his window perch, is that not so?"

"Oh, I'm sorry but I refuse to believe such a thing; it is absolutely inconceivable to me."

"However," Wolfe said, "here we have an arguably eccentric woman given to at least occasional outbursts of choler who also is far younger and substantially larger than your father."

"I say that is just plain nonsense," Nadia persisted, finally showing a spark of independence. "Besides, I have no idea whether Zondra ever even visited Daddy in that dumpy old office of his. I can't imagine any reason why she would have gone there."

"Very well," Wolfe said. "Let us now discuss your father's wife."

"Alexis?" Nadia said sharply, wrinkling her nose. "Whatever for?"

"Might she have pushed her husband from his urban perch?"

"She is a lot of things, many of which I don't like, but I really can't believe that being a murderess is one of them."

"What don't you like about her?"

"Where to start? For one thing, she is as cold as ice. As I think I've told you before, I don't know what Daddy ever saw in her. She and I had little contact from the very beginning, which was fine with me. She didn't like me any more than I liked her."

"How did your father feel about the animosity that existed between the two of you?"

Nadia shrugged. "At first, he tried to play the role of peace-maker, but he quickly realized that wasn't going to work and he gave up. He soon realized that the only times he was going to see me was when Alexis wasn't around, so we would meet for lunch or sometimes dinner away from their home on those times when I was in the city from school. And when I was in town, I bedded down at the home of a classmate's parents in Brooklyn. I never, not once, stayed in the town house with Daddy and Alexis."

"Do you know there is a rumor circulating that you pushed your father off that windowsill?" Wolfe murmured.

"That is outrageous!" Nadia snapped, leaning forward and clenching her small fists. "Do you believe it?"

"I do not, Miss Wordell."

"Well, at least I am happy to hear *that*," she said, on the verge of hyperventilating. "I would not be surprised if such garbage— and that's what it is—originated with Alexis herself."

"Did she resent you because she thought you would inherit your father's estate?" Wolfe asked.

"Oh, that is probably a part of it, all right, although our law-yer, Daddy's and mine, tells me that because they still were married, she might be entitled to some of the estate, since there is no will that anyone has yet been able to locate."

"How would you feel if the widow were to receive a substantial portion of your father's estate?"

Nadia had begun to calm down, although she still was tense and sat on the edge of the chair. "I don't think it would be fair, but I am not by nature a fighter; it is simply not in my makeup. I suppose I would accept a court's ruling, if it was to come to that."

"Very well," Wolfe said, draining the last of his beer and getting to his feet. "I believe we have covered all the ground we are likely to today. I have another engagement. Miss Wordell, you will be hearing from Mr. Goodwin." With that, he walked out.

Hewitt chuckled, as if to reassure Nadia. "Nero Wolfe has never mastered the art of the graceful exit," he said. "In fact, I doubt if he's even tried, right?" he added, turning to me.

"Bull's-eye," I replied. "Nadia, please do not take offense at Mr. Wolfe's brusque demeanor, or his interrogation techniques, for that matter. He has never taken the time, nor the interest, to practice some of the social niceties that most of us observe. For better or worse, that is one part of the price that you pay when you are dealing with a genius."

"I understand," she said, putting a slender hand on my arm, "and I assure you that I am not in any way offended. Keep in mind that my father was hardly what you would call an advocate of the Emily Post school of manners. And he was a genius of sorts himself."

I saw them both to the front door and echoed Wolfe's words that they would be hearing from me.

CHAPTER 14

That other "engagement" Wolfe referred to, as you no doubt have figured out, was in the kitchen. There he would be supervising Fritz's work on dinner, which was to be lobster in white wine sauce. During these premeal conferences, an argument often occurs, and I make it a point to stay away from the action, lest I get hit with a flying onion thrown in Wolfe's direction by Fritz.

After lunch, as we sat in the office with coffee, I turned to Wolfe. "Well, you certainly took Nadia Wordell through her paces this morning and shook the young woman up. Do you feel you learned anything?"

"Not as much as I would have wished. She still remains hesitant to point fingers. Perhaps we will make some progress in our meetings with Mr. Tatum and Miss Zagreb. Have you set up times for them to be here?"

"Yes, sir, and following your orders, as I invariably do, I have arranged for Tatum to be here at nine tonight and Zondra at nine tomorrow night. They both seemed pleased to have been invited, and Tatum in particular acted like he was eager to talk to you."

"I was not aware that you invariably follow what I prefer to call directives rather than orders," Wolfe said. "And strictly speaking, the two in effect have invited themselves."

"All right, since you prefer to split hairs. But however you choose to term their visits, they will be here." Wolfe's response was not to thank me for my efforts, but rather to bury his head in his latest book.

Boyd Tatum arrived at the brownstone several minutes before nine, and he looked just as I remembered him from that Waldorf Astoria dinner: rumpled, short, slightly paunchy, and with a self-deprecating smile and a shock of salt-and-pepper hair that kept falling over one eye. Central casting could not have come up with a better model for a professor at a prestigious university, including the pipe whose bowl protruded from his tweed jacket's breast pocket. A cynic might suggest that he was trying too hard to create an image.

"Ah, you of course are Mr. Goodwin," Tatum said as he stepped in. "I remember you from that dinner where we were tablemates, and you were with the lovely Miss Rowan. How is she?"

I responded that Lily was fine and steered the professor down the hall to the office, where Wolfe was flipping the pages of a world atlas. "Good evening, sir," he said. "Can we get you something to drink? As you see, I am having beer."

"Would scotch and soda be available?" Tatum asked, grinning and brushing the hair back from his forehead. Wolfe nodded in my direction, and I went to the drink table against the wall and filled the order while our guest settled into the red leather chair.

"It is very kind of you to see me on such short notice," Tatum said. "Have any other friends of Arthur come to see you?"

"You are the first," Wolfe replied.

"Interesting. I'd have thought several of them would want to meet with you when they learned that you are looking into his death."

"Perhaps they feel that they have nothing to contribute to my investigation. Do you, sir?"

Tatum smiled and took a sip of his drink. "I am not sure that I do, Mr. Wolfe, although I have some thoughts."

"Share them with Mr. Goodwin and me."

"I have done a lot of thinking since that terrible night when Arthur fell to his death. I must assume you do not believe that what occurred in that building was an accident."

"Assume what you will, sir. I have been hired to ascertain the cause of death, be it misfortune or murder."

"May I ask who your client is?" Tatum asked with a smile.

"You may, but it will be to no avail."

"Of course, of course; yours I am sure is akin to a lawyer-client relationship. I was off base in asking and I withdraw the question."

"It is of no matter," Wolfe said, flipping a palm. "Have you come to us with any information that might be of assistance? You said you have done a lot of thinking since Mr. Wordell's death."

"That's true, I have. And I remain absolutely convinced that Arthur's fall was an accident, a mishap if you will."

"Had you visited him often in that Midtown building?"

"Only once, and I did not like the place at all. I have never understood why he insisted on picking those seedy quarters as a so-called office, especially when he had a much nicer arrangement at his home on the Upper East Side."

"It has been said of the man that he liked to sit on that window ledge and savor the sights and sounds of the city below."

Tatum rolled his eyes and nodded. "Yes, I have heard all about that. Arthur, despite his curmudgeonly exterior, was something of a romantic, although I suppose he would have been appalled by that description of him. He was a true eccentric as well, and he did love the city. But I also feel that he was mentally unbalanced, and it concerns me that this investigation may turn into a circus for the press, which seems to be always looking for circuses."

"That remains a possibility," Wolfe conceded, "but being a longtime acquaintance of Mr. Wordell, you must want to see justice done, if I may employ an overused phrase."

"Oh, yes, I suppose I do." Tatum sighed and took a healthy drink of his scotch. "I would just hate for his daughter, who is a charming and somewhat fragile young woman, to have to go through a constant rehashing of her father's death by the newspapers and radio and television stations, and now—please do not take offense—by you as well."

"None taken," Wolfe said. "How did you and Mr. Wordell know each other?"

"It has been some years ago now, probably ten or more," the professor said, leaning back and pressing his palms over his eyes. "Arthur called me at the university and asked my opinion about a Monet that was part of a collection being auctioned. I was familiar with the oil and told him I felt it was one of the artist's finest works. At first, I was puzzled as to why he would call me, and then I realized he probably had read a monograph of mine on Monet. Arthur ended up buying the painting, and then he ended up buying me lunch, as a kind of thanks, I suppose."

"And that was the first face-to-face meeting you had?"

"Yes, it was, Mr. Wolfe. And over the next few years, he asked my opinion on several more occasions, and I always gave him what I felt was good advice as to whether to bid on a piece of art—or to not bid on it. And I'm pleased to say that he usually took my advice."

"I understand that more recently you had wanted to write a tome about Mr. Wordell and his art collection," Wolfe said.

Tatum eyed his glass, now empty, which I took to the cart for a refill. "Yes, as you may know, I have written a number of books, articles, and monographs about art connoisseurs and their collections. I hope I am not sounding overly vain, but I have been praised for my work in this area, both at New York University and in the world beyond the groves of academia. I had hoped to get Arthur to agree to be one of my subjects, and I had a publisher lined up who was most interested and who I'm pleased to say offered me an advance. Because of the help I had been to him on numerous occasions, I felt he would agree."

"What was Mr. Wordell's reaction to your proposal?"

"Oh, he was far less than enthusiastic, I can assure you of that," Tatum said, shaking his head as if in disbelief. "Arthur has always been known for his love of privacy, but I felt that as a friend of some years, I could persuade him to sit still for interviews and a detailed description of how he came to amass his wonderful collection. Sadly, I was proven incorrect."

"Did this contretemps cause a rift in your relationship?"

Tatum's cheeks colored, although that may have been the result of the single-malt scotch he had rather quickly ingested. "Well, I guess it is fair to say that I was not very happy with Arthur's reaction to my proposal, and the fact that he felt I had attempted to take advantage of our relationship."

"I believe a magazine that deals with the fine arts had once planned to run an article on Mr. Wordell and his collection."

"Yes, that's right, *Art & Artists*, Emory Sterling's publication," Tatum said, bitterness creeping into his tone. "The piece never ran because of Arthur's objections over its content, and I understand that it caused some friction between the two of them. That whole episode also certainly did not help my cause."

"How would you describe your relationship with Mr. Wordell at the time of his death?" Wolfe asked.

"I truly wish that it had been better," Tatum said with a sigh. "So should I then assume that you are going to continue your investigation, determined to find a murderer?"

"I will most surely continue my investigation, sir, determined to unearth the truth, whatever it may be."

"I don't know whether to wish you well or not," the professor said, forcing a smile and rising to leave. "Mr. Goodwin, thank you for the scotch. It was as fine as any I have ever had. Now it's back to my abode in Greenwich Village. Good night to you both."

"That was a somewhat abrupt departure by our rather urbane academic," I told Wolfe when I returned to the office after watching Boyd Tatum go down the steps of the brownstone and set off in search of a southbound cab.

"For whatever reasons, the gentleman would seem to prefer that we drop our quest," Wolfe said.

"It could be that the professorial Mr. Tatum shoved Wordell off that window ledge himself."

"A possibility of course, Archie. Or perhaps he suspects someone else did the shoving and is trying, albeit in a ham-handed way, to protect that individual, for whatever reason."

"Well, you now have almost twenty-four hours to prepare yourself for the arrival on our doorstep of Zondra Zagreb, artist extraordinaire."

Wolfe scowled. "One would think if she did not like her birth name she could have chosen a better one for her public persona."

"At least it's alliterative," I said, "and I believe I'm using that word correctly. After all, I learned it from you."

"It is comforting to know that at least some of what is directed at you finds its mark," Wolfe replied as he picked up an orchid catalog and began reading.

CHAPTER 15

I was not looking forward to Zondra's visit, as I had no idea how she would be dressed. If her garb was anywhere near what she wore to the Waldorf dinner, Wolfe would likely bolt the moment she stepped into the office.

As it turned out, I need not have been concerned in that respect. When I answered the bell at a few minutes before nine the next night and swung open the front door, I found myself facing a smiling and primly clad Miss Zagreb. Okay, nothing could be done about the blond crew cut, this time dyed an Easter-egg blue, but otherwise she was the picture of respectability: a gray cowl-necked sweater; black midlength skirt; and no-nonsense black pumps.

"Are you surprised at my appearance, Archie Goodwin?" she asked with a wink as she stepped in. Before I could mount a reply, she continued.

"From what I have learned about Nero Wolfe, courtesy of your friend Lily, he definitely would not approve of my, well . . . *usual* mode of dress, so I decided to dig deeply into my closet and come up with something that might be more proper, given the circumstances tonight. I haven't been garbed this demurely in years."

"A wise choice," I replied as I escorted her down the hall to the office. "Miss Zagreb, this is Nero Wolfe. Please have a seat."

"Madam," Wolfe said, glancing at her hair and dipping his chin a quarter of an inch. "Would you like Mr. Goodwin to get you something to drink?"

"No, thank you," she answered, easing herself into the red leather chair, legs together and hands folded in her lap, a truly modest picture. *Don't overdo it, lady*, I thought.

"You wish to see me concerning the death of Mr. Wordell?" Wolfe said.

"Yes. I have of course read that you are investigating what happened, and I thought I should offer my thoughts, for what they may be worth."

"Please do."

Zondra took a deep breath and leaned forward. "I don't know what you may have heard about my relationship with Arthur, but I am aware of your reputation, Mr. Wolfe, so I realize that you are bound to learn things about me if you haven't already." She turned to me, her face tensed. "Might I take you up on that drink now?" she said, clearing her throat. "I would like a bourbon and water with ice, please, if it is not too much trouble."

"No trouble at all," I told her, moving to the cart against the wall and playing bartender. She thanked me with a voice just above a whisper and accepted the glass. This was a far more subdued and somber individual than I had seen on two earlier occasions, and I was about to find out why.

She took a sip of the drink and turned back to Wolfe. "Arthur and I were . . . I guess you would call us an *item* . . . for two, well, almost three years," she said, her face coloring. "I am pretty sure very few people were aware of it. I don't think even Nadia knew anything, that's how private we were."

Wolfe frowned. He is always uncomfortable with what might be termed affairs of the heart. "Were you and Mr. Wordell still engaged in this liaison at the time of his death?" he asked.

"Oh, no, that ended almost six months ago now."

"Who, or what, led to the fissure in the relationship?"

"Oh, Arthur ended it, and just like that," Zondra replied, snapping her fingers. "As I am sure you know, he was not the warmest of men, and he could change course very quickly. Well, he sure changed course where I was concerned. It was, 'bye, bye baby,' so to speak, before you could even blink."

"What precipitated Mr. Wordell's decision?"

"I wish I could tell you. I really don't believe he felt that I was a fortune hunter, because I have been able to support myself very nicely through the sales of my work, which has been generally well reviewed. If that sounds like I am blowing my own horn, I am sorry, but you can ask around in the arts community as to my reputation."

I felt that Zondra could use a little support, so I cut in, addressing my remarks to Wolfe. "Lily Rowan, who does a good bit of art collecting herself, told me she thinks Miss Zagreb's work is better than that done by others, some of them famous, who are working in the same style as she." For my efforts, I got a smile from the artist and no reaction from my boss.

"Did Mr. Wordell appreciate your artistic abilities?" Wolfe asked.

"I was never quite sure about that. Oh, on occasion he would say a few complimentary words, but never anything that I would consider to be effusive. He tended to save his most lavish praise for the artists whose work he collected, almost all of them of course being world famous. I think at least part of the reason he was drawn to me was that I amused him and could make him laugh, something he otherwise did not do very often at all."

I cut in again. "I saw an example of that at the Waldorf dinner," I told Wolfe. "Miss Zagreb teased Wordell, asking if he thought her art belonged in the new Guggenheim museum, and she actually got a smile and a chuckle out of the old boy, which I gather was something of a rarity for him. It was about the only smiling he did that night."

"And that was well after our . . . involvement, was over," she said, looking down at her lap. "But I was still very fond of Arthur and really did like to joke with him. And he seemed to enjoy it, too."

"Does Lily know anything about what you refer to as your 'involvement'?" I asked.

"No, nobody does, at least as far as I know, although you never can be sure. We only ever saw each other at his home on the Upper East Side, and once at a small and quiet restaurant up near the Columbia campus. We felt that even in the unlikely event that someone we knew happened to come upon us there, we could say we were discussing art and artists."

"Why have you come to me, Miss Zagreb?" Wolfe asked sharply.

"As I said earlier, I have heard about your reputation for thoroughness, and I felt that somehow the close friendship I had with Arthur might eventually come out. And because of how that friendship ended, it is possible I would be seen as a possible suspect in his death."

Wolfe considered her through half-lidded eyes. "Do you have any thoughts as to how Mr. Wordell died?"

She took several seconds to respond. "I have to believe that he was pushed."

"Do you have a candidate?"

Another pause. "I knew you would ask that, of course."

"Of course."

"I am sorry, Mr. Wolfe, but I simply cannot conceive of anyone I know having . . . having done that to Arthur."

"But you repeat that you think he was pushed and did not leave his perch on that windowsill accidentally?"

"Yes, yes, I do."

"So, it would seem that your sole purpose in coming here has been to establish that you had a close relationship to Mr. Wordell, and in so doing make it appear that you have nothing whatever to hide."

"But that's just it; I *don't* have anything to hide!" Zondra snapped.

"Perhaps. But it appears both you and the late Mr. Wordell went to a great deal of effort to make sure your amour went undiscovered."

That seemed to stymie the lady, who once again was mute for several seconds, clearly trying to collect her thoughts. "I feel like I am being interrogated," she said, her voice beginning to crack.

"Madam, you requested this meeting, did you not?"

She nodded.

"What did you expect? I am a detective, I ask questions, I seek answers. And so far, I have been less than successful with you. Let us move on: How and when did you and Arthur Wordell meet?"

Zondra shifted in her chair and pursed her lips as if deep in thought. "It was, uh . . . about six years ago now. I attended an auction at a dealer's up near the Metropolitan Museum because

I knew one of the artists and was curious as to how her work would sell. Arthur was there, bidding on a Renoir and a Lautrec, both of which he got, as usual. He was a very aggressive bidder, as you probably know. Anyway, I was sitting next to him by chance, and he started talking to me. I knew right away he was interested in me. That didn't take a genius to realize.

"After a little small talk, which he really was not very good at, he asked about my own art, probably just to be polite. Then he suggested I might like to see some of his collection at his town house in the Eighties."

"The old 'come on up to my place and see my etchings' approach," I said.

Zondra laughed nervously. "When you put it that way, the line seems pretty obvious, doesn't it?" she said, shaking her head. "I never saw myself as being naive, but to be honest, I found Arthur attractive, despite his age."

"And as you told us before, this relationship went on for between two and three years?" Wolfe asked.

She nodded.

"Do you have any idea why he ended it so abruptly?"

"I really don't," she said. "There was never any kind of a quarrel, or even a minor difference of opinion."

"Thank you for coming," Wolfe said. "Archie will see you out."

"I am so sorry to have wasted your time," Zondra said with a sniff, standing and pivoting toward the doorway. "I see that coming here was a mistake on my part, a total mistake." She walked out and went down the hall with me a step behind her.

"Would you like me to hail a cab for you?" I asked at the front door.

"No, thank you, Archie Goodwin, I am quite capable of doing that myself." To say her tone was icy would be an understatement. She walked down our front steps and went in the direction of Tenth Avenue, where she would presumably get a northbound taxi. She kept her eyes straight ahead.

Back in the office, I sat at my desk and turned to Wolfe, but before I could say anything, he spoke.

"Was that woman gulling me?" There we were again, my boss turning to me for advice on how to read a woman.

"Gulling you—maybe. That was pretty cute the way she brought up her affair, though."

"Cute? Bah! It was a puerile attempt to make her seem totally transparent by confessing to something before we learned of it from another source—if indeed we would have. Do you think Miss Rowan knows anything of this relationship the artist referred to?"

"I very much doubt it, or I believe she would have said something to me. She usually tells me everything, at least when it involves a case we are working on. What is our next move?"

"I am mildly disappointed we have not heard from any of Mr. Wordell's other close associates. I had hoped the *Gazette* article would bring more responses, but so be it. We will talk in the morning."

CHAPTER 16

As it turned out, by the time Wolfe and I did talk the next morning, we had plenty to discuss. I sat in the office with coffee after breakfast when the phone rang, and I answered in the usual way.

"Ah, yes, Mr. Archie Goodwin. You may not remember me. My name is Emory Sterling."

"Of course, I remember you. We sat at the same table at that Waldorf Astoria dinner a while back."

"And you were accompanied by the lovely and most engaging Miss Lily Rowan, making you the envy of all the men at the table, and probably throughout that entire room as well."

"I had better not tell her that you said that; she has more than enough self-confidence as it is."

"And with good reason," Sterling said with a laugh. "The reason I am telephoning is that I would like to see Nero Wolfe, and I have learned enough about him to realize that he rarely leaves his home. That being the case, I am willing to come to his office at a time that is mutually agreeable."

"Before we get ahead of ourselves, I'll need to tell Mr. Wolfe the reason for your visit."

"I am aware of course that he has been investigating Arthur Wordell's death, and I would like to offer my thoughts, for what they may be worth."

"Mr. Wolfe is not available at present, but when he is, I will give him your message," I said, getting Sterling's phone number and promising he would hear from me before the day was out.

No more than five minutes later, the telephone squawked again. The deep voice at the other end introduced himself by saying, "I am Henry Banks, Mr. Goodwin. You may or may not remember having met me."

"I do happen to remember very well, sir, in a very large and very crowded hotel ballroom."

"Ah, yes, that was quite an evening, was it not?"

"Quite an evening," I agreed, wondering where this conversation was headed. "How may I help you, Mr. Banks?"

"Your employer, Nero Wolfe—is he by any chance available?"

"Not at the moment. May I take a message?"

"Well, I have read that he, Mr. Wolfe, is investigating the death of my dear friend Arthur Wordell, and I, well . . . was hoping I might be able to talk to him about what he has been able to learn regarding this tragic business."

"I will leave him a note that you called," I said, getting the number where he could be reached. "Is there anything else?"

"No, nothing, Mr. Goodwin. Am I likely to hear back from Mr. Wolfe?"

"That I cannot answer, but I assure you that he will receive your message this morning."

Banks started to reply but realized there was nothing more for him to say. He cleared his throat and muttered a "thank-you" before hanging up.

The elevator descended at two or three minutes after eleven as it always does, marking the end of Wolfe's morning séance with his orchids. He strode into the office with a raceme of purple orchids and placed it in a thin vase on his desk, then asked if I had slept well.

I replied in the affirmative, and as he settled into his desk chair and rang for beer, I turned to him and asked: "Do you think the office is bugged?"

"What kind is flummery is this?" he demanded.

"Last night, you said you were disappointed at not having heard from more of the late Mr. Wordell's friends—or maybe acquaintances would be a more accurate term. Well, this morning, within a five-minute span, two of these acquaintances of his telephoned, and each of them has requested an audience with you. Seems like more than a coincidence."

"Confound it, report."

"Yes, sir. The first call came from Emory Sterling, he of the presumably prestigious arts magazine, who says that he is willing to share his thoughts about Arthur Wordell's death. I did not press him for details and said we would get back to him. Next came Henry Banks, the gentleman who, like Sterling, has been on Wordell's advisory board and was formerly the curator of some private art collections. He seems very curious to learn how your investigation is progressing."

I did not expect this news to elate Wolfe, but I felt he would at least get some satisfaction from it. It appears that I was wrong, as he scowled after my brief summary.

"Do you want me to set up some times for you to see these two gentlemen?" I asked.

Wolfe took the day's first drink of beer and set his glass down, licking his lips. "All right," he said with a sigh, resigned to the fact that he would have to go back to work. He knew very well that I would keep after him until he took some sort of action, but as I mentioned earlier, such was a big part of why I was hired in the first place: to be a burr under his saddle.

"See if Mr. Sterling can come at three today and Mr. Banks at nine."

"Two in one day? Fine by me. Any other instructions?"

"None," he said, going through the mail I had opened and stacked on his desk blotter. I got lucky twice. I reached Sterling on the first try, and he seemed happy to show up on such short notice. Banks also answered and said he could be at the brownstone at nine.

Emory Sterling was prompt and was as I remembered him: tall, immaculately tailored in a three-piece glen plaid suit, immaculately barbered with center-parted graying hair, and the picture of confidence. He looked as if he could have just stepped off the pages of *Gentlemen's Quarterly*.

"Mr. Goodwin, it is so good to see you again," he said, doffing his homburg and coat and handing them to me. "I am looking forward to meeting the legendary Nero Wolfe."

"I hope that he lives up to your expectations," I said. "This way to the inner sanctum." I led him down the hall to the office, where Wolfe looked up from his desk, nodded, and asked if Sterling wanted anything to drink. Our guest declined with thanks and settled into the red leather chair.

"The floor is yours, Mr. Sterling," Wolfe said.

"Thank you for agreeing to see me," the magazine owner and publisher said. "I may or I may not have some information regarding your investigation into Arthur Wordell's death."

Wolfe nodded, the signal for Sterling to proceed. Our guest crossed his legs, cleared his throat, and steepled his hands, as if in contemplation. "I want to be very careful with what I say, lest it be misconstrued."

"Conversations in this room are confidential unless directly related to the commission of a criminal activity. And I assure you that Mr. Goodwin is every bit as tight-lipped as I am. Anything considered too confidential for him would find me deaf."

"Understood. Before I begin, I would like to ask if you feel you have made progress in determining the cause of Arthur's death."

"You may ask, sir, but I am not inclined to answer."

"Ah, yes, I of course should not have posed the question," Sterling said. "As I know that you are well aware, I am one of three persons Arthur asked to be on a board to advise him about his superb collection. Although he never told any of us in so many words, he apparently had lost confidence in Roger Mason, who has been the collection's curator."

"I am indeed aware you had been a member of that troika," Wolfe said.

"The funny thing is, we have never formally met en masse, not even once. Arthur invariably had sessions with each of us separately, and at least speaking for myself, I am not sure that I contributed very much. Arthur had his own very definite ideas about what he wanted done with his art. I cannot for the life of me figure out why he formed an advisory board at all, unless it was to spite Roger."

"Why would he want to do that?"

Sterling wrinkled his patrician brow. "I honestly don't know, but the two of them had a somewhat stormy relationship, which is part of the reason I had asked to see you."

"Continue," Wolfe said, interlacing his fingers over his center mound.

"About two months ago—I can get you the exact date if you like—Arthur invited me to his town house on the Upper East Side to discuss his collection. When I got there, the butler put me in the library and explained that Arthur was in conference in his office across the hall.

"The ancient butler inadvertently left the library door ajar, and even though Arthur's office door was closed, I could hear voices inside that gradually became louder. I eventually recognized one of those voices—Roger Mason—and his words came through clearly. He said, 'Dammit, Arthur, it would give me great pleasure to strangle you.' Arthur responded in an angry tone himself, although I could not hear clearly what he said."

"Words spoken in anger are not always the best barometer of a relationship," Wolfe observed.

"Perhaps not," Sterling responded, nodding. "Although given what I have heard from others, this was by no means the only time the two men had exchanged unpleasant words."

"Which raises the question as to why Mr. Wordell chose Roger Mason to work with his collection in the first place."

"Roger is justifiably respected in the world of fine art," Sterling said. "He had been the director of a pair of well-regarded New England art museums. When I heard he had been named to oversee Arthur's collection, I mentally applauded the choice, having no idea at the time that the two would butt horns."

"And what caused them to butt horns?" Wolfe asked.

"I wish I knew. Of course, Arthur could be more than a little acerbic, or maybe cantankerous is a better word. When dealing with him, I found diplomacy to be the best course, and apparently Roger has the tendency to speak his mind and not sugarcoat his opinions, regardless of whom he is talking to."

"I happen to subscribe to that approach myself," Wolfe said, "but I understand such a method can be perilous when dealing with certain individuals."

"Including Wordell," Sterling replied ruefully.

"How would you describe your own relationship with Arthur Wordell?" Wolfe asked.

"A lot more amiable than the Wordell-Mason pairing, although far from perfect."

"Did you ever have occasion to cross swords with the collector?"

Sterling rubbed his palms together before speaking. "Well . . . I am not sure this qualifies as 'crossing swords,' but we did have a marked difference of opinion on one occasion a few years ago. I had suggested to the staff at *Arts & Artists* that we do a profile of Arthur that would of course highlight his collection but also would discuss his philosophy of collecting as well. He told me in no uncertain terms that he was not interested and would not cooperate or be quoted. One of my writers went ahead and wrote the piece without his help. I then showed Arthur the article, and he became angry with what was written. I argued with him, but it was to no avail."

"Were you surprised at the intensity of his reaction?" Wolfe asked.

"Yes and no," Sterling said. "I was aware that he had refused to be quoted in a *New York Times* article about his collection, so I was aware that he could be difficult. But because of our long-time friendship—I once acted as a go-between to help Arthur purchase a Kandinsky from a reclusive and reluctant owner— I felt that he would surely cooperate. As it turned out, I was wrong, and I then had to inform the magazine's editors that there would be no feature on Arthur. And this after I had all but assured the staff that I could persuade him to cooperate."

"But that episode did not permanently damage your relationship?"

"Well . . . no, I do not believe it did, although in truth, relations were quite cool between us for some time after the episode. I am not one for holding grudges, and apparently Arthur isn't either, because had that been the case, he certainly would not have asked me to be on that advisory board—the board that really did not do all that much advising," Sterling said with a strained laugh, shaking his head.

"What were your thoughts on where the Wordell art should repose?"

"I was not as big an enthusiast of Arthur's works going to the Guggenheim as Roger Mason and some others have been. I rather liked the idea of various parts of his collection going to different museums—museums that specialized in particular genres or eras."

"In other words, match the art to the museum?"

"Yes, that is it exactly, Mr. Wolfe. But Arthur seemed lukewarm—no, far less than lukewarm—to my idea. And when I broached it to him, he let me know in plain terms that he did not like it one bit. He made it clear there would be no further discussion on the matter."

"You mentioned earlier that Mr. Wordell had definite ideas as to the disposition of his art. Can you elucidate?"

Sterling shifted in his chair. "Arthur really seemed adamant in desiring that his collection be kept together, which of course meant that he rejected my suggestion out of hand."

"Did that decision bother you?"

"Oh, no, not really," the publisher said. "After all, these were his possessions, and he had every right to decide where they were to find a home. However, even though he wanted the collection kept intact, he did not like it at all when people assumed that as a matter of course they would go to the Guggenheim."

"I saw an example of that at the Waldorf dinner," I interjected. "Wordell flared up when that emcee made it sound like it was a given that his collection was headed for the new museum."

"Exactly!" Sterling said, slapping a palm down on the arm of his chair. "I really thought he was going to walk out at that moment. And I believe he would have if Nadia hadn't begged him to stay. She may be somewhat shy and reserved, but her father did pay attention to her opinions, and in this case her entreaty. My belief is that Arthur had planned to make an announcement about the collection going to the Guggenheim when he was good and ready, and he did not want anyone to upstage him."

"Is there anything else you care to add regarding Mr. Wordell and his death?" Wolfe posed.

"No . . . nothing, just that it was a terrible tragedy, and a great loss to the art world, as I have told his daughter. Although any words from me would be of scant solace to Nadia. Do I gather that you have no further need of me?"

"Before you leave, sir, I would be interested in learning how you first encountered Mr. Wordell."

"Oh my, that must have been at least fifteen years ago, maybe slightly longer," Sterling said. "I had just started *Art & Artists*, and shortly after the first issue came out, Arthur telephoned me to say that he was pleased that somebody was introducing a new publication. I can still hear his words: 'It's about time we had a new voice in town that discusses the art world with intelligence.' From then on, we corresponded or talked on the telephone from time to time. He often had suggestions—and usually good ones—for possible topics. And on occasion, he also would be critical of an article, sometimes with good reason. I came to consider him a friend, both of mine and of the publication."

"Do you have anything else to add?"

"I don't think so, other than to say I have a hard time believing Arthur's fall was an accident."

"Would you nominate someone as his murderer?"

Sterling pondered the question. "Frankly, I can't think of anyone I know who disliked him enough to kill him, not even Roger Mason, despite the animosity between the two and despite what I heard that day in Arthur's residence. I guess I just don't see the motive."

"Thank you for coming," Wolfe said, which our guest realized was the cue for him to leave. He rose, nodded to each of us, and left the room, heading down the hall to the front door.

"Well, what do you think?" I asked when I got back to the office after seeing Emory Sterling out.

"A man who chooses his words judiciously. He would have made an excellent ambassador to any one of several European countries," Wolfe observed.

"What about that threat from Mason?"

"It is certainly worth keeping in mind," Wolfe said, checking his pocket watch. In three minutes, he would board the elevator for his afternoon visit to the orchids.

CHAPTER 17

As a rule, Nero Wolfe tries to avoid conducting one-on-one interviews twice in the same day. But he needs a steady infusion of money to pay for all his comforts, including orchids, beer by the case, gourmet food, at least ten new books a month, the services of one grumpy old orchid nurse, Theodore Horstmann, one world-class chef, Fritz Brenner, and one all-purpose dogsbody—me. If you don't know what that phrase means, just look it up, which I had to do myself after someone used it to describe me.

The only way that Wolfe is going to haul in money at the rate he spends it is by solving crimes for clients who can afford his exorbitant rates, and the only way he is going to solve crimes is by talking to people. Hence, this was to be a two-interview day, whether or not he liked it—and he definitely did not.

A light rain had begun falling when Henry Banks arrived at our front door a few minutes before nine that night. "Come in out of the weather," I told him, taking his umbrella and putting it in the stand next to the coat rack.

"Thank you, Mr. Goodwin," he said, holding out a hand, which I took. Banks looked the same as he had at the Waldorf dinner: stocky, well nourished, and outwardly eager to please. I directed him down the hall to the office, into which he cautiously stepped, gazing around at the room at its appointments and then at Nero Wolfe. "A very nice room," he said with a smile. "I must say that it looks extremely comfortable."

"It suits my needs very nicely, sir, despite what one self-absorbed architect thinks of it."

"That sounds suspiciously like you are referring to one Frank Lloyd Wright," Banks said with a smile as he plopped into the red leather chair and continued to look around the room. "Has he by chance been here?"

"Yes, he has," Wolfe replied, "but it is of no matter. His opinions do not concern me in the least."

"I feel the same way, even though he is said by many to be a genius. Thank you for taking the time to see me."

Wolfe asked if our guest would like a drink, and he declined politely, clearing his throat. "I am of course curious as to how your investigation into Arthur's death proceeds," he said, leaning forward and resting his elbows on his knees.

"It proceeds," Wolfe replied. "Have you anything to contribute?"

"I am not sure that I have, although I continue to find it hard to believe that Arthur's fall from that window ledge was an accident."

"Can you suggest anyone whose animus toward Mr. Wordell was of such intensity that he or she could have dispatched him?"

Banks cleared his throat again, which seemed to be standard procedure whenever he began to speak. "I cannot conceive of anyone who I know having . . . well, having done something violent to Arthur."

"But yet you say you do not think his fatal plunge was an accident."

More throat clearing. "I do not, Mr. Wolfe. I wish that I could be of some help to you."

"That being the case, sir, I must say I am curious as to why you requested this meeting."

"Well, I suppose it was curiosity more than anything else, curiosity as to what you have been able to learn."

Wolfe leaned back and considered our guest. "Mr. Banks, how would you describe your own relationship with Arthur Wordell?"

"I like to think that we were good friends, at least as good as anyone could be with Arthur. As you probably are aware, he was not the easiest person to get close to, although I worked hard to be his friend."

"How did he feel about you?"

Banks shrugged narrow shoulders. "Well, he did ask me to be part of that advisory group, which tells me that he respected my opinions about art and artists."

"How long had you known Mr. Wordell?"

"More than ten years now. We first met at the home of a man up in Westchester County for whose private collection I had served as an adviser. Arthur had wanted to purchase one of his works, a landscape by Van Gogh, and my friend wanted me to be present at their meeting to counsel him. Arthur ended up buying the Van Gogh, and both men seemed happy with the price, which I helped to negotiate.

" 'I like the way you operate,' Arthur told me later. 'You acted in your friend's best interests, but at the same time you did not try to hold me up in the process. You were an honest broker, and it seems to me that everyone got what they wanted.' I really believe that episode is why Arthur asked me to be part of his advisory board."

"How often did that group meet?"

"Well now, there's the funny thing," he said, rubbing his chin. "We never, not even once, met as a committee of the whole. He would see each of us separately to ask our opinions about his collection and what he felt he should do with it."

"What was your advice?" Wolfe asked.

Banks leaned forward and waited several seconds before answering. "I told him that I thought he should loan or bequeath the collection, or at least the bulk of it, to the Guggenheim. It seemed to me that the new museum would be a great showcase for his art."

"What was his reaction to that?"

"Arthur had earlier said that he liked the new museum, but after he looked at architectural drawings of the interior, he said to me, 'I'm not sure that I like that spiral walkway of Wright's, or whatever he's calling it. Should people be looking at art while standing on a slant? What if they have dizzy spells, for heaven's sake?' "

"How did you respond to that observation?"

"I told him, as diplomatically as I could, that I thought that visitors would quickly adapt to this new concept in art museum design. I personally found it to be exciting and revolutionary."

"Even though you say you are not enthusiastic about Mr. Wright."

"As an individual, no, I definitely am not," Banks said with feeling. "He has what I would term unbridled arrogance. But I reluctantly recognize that he is a visionary, and his design for the Guggenheim is both radical and groundbreaking. I felt that Arthur's collection belonged there for maximum impact."

"Where did your meetings with Mr. Wordell take place?"

"Occasionally at his home on the Upper East Side, but more often in that crazy office of his in Midtown, the place where he . . . well, you know . . ."

"Did he conduct any of those sessions with you while he was seated on that sill with the window open?" Wolfe asked.

Banks nodded, wearing a rueful smile. "Yes, which I found strange, to say the least, especially since he had to look over his shoulder to see me when we talked. But for some reason I can't explain, I never felt that he was in any sort of danger. Now me, I could no more sit there like he did with his legs dangling than I could make myself ride on one of those horrid roller coasters out at Coney Island. Just looking at them makes me nauseated."

"Let us return to the advisory board. Do you know what the stimulus was for Mr. Wordell to create it?"

Banks seemed uncomfortable and squirmed in the chair. "He . . . thought that he needed some new ideas as to how to best exhibit his collection."

"But didn't he already have a curator?"

"He did, but, well . . . Arthur never seemed satisfied with Roger. For that matter, I don't think he was ever satisfied with what those of us on the advisory board suggested to him. The man was a contrarian by his very nature."

"Do you have any explanation as to why your board never met with him as a whole?"

"Oh dear, you do ask the most formidable questions, don't you? My theory, for what it's worth, is that Arthur liked to play people off against one another, and he could do it more easily by seeing them one-on-one. I am by no means a psychologist, but I do think because of something in his nature, he derived a perverse pleasure from telling each of us that one or more of the others on the board had a diametrically opposed view."

"What is your opinion of Roger Mason?" Wolfe asked.

"As an individual or in his professional capacity?"

"Both." Wolfe was keeping the heat on our guest.

"Roger was extremely knowledgeable about art, and not just any single genre. He could expound on everything from the Italian Renaissance and the Dutch Masters to impressionism and Dadaism with equal facility. I have heard several of his lectures, and they exhibited nothing short of brilliant scholarship and knowledge."

"What of the man?"

I believe that at that moment, Henry Banks would have rather been anywhere but in the old brownstone on West Thirty-Fifth Street over near the Hudson. This time, he treated us to an extended clearing of the throat. "I just do not like to speak ill of people," he finally said.

"In an ideal world, that is an exemplary position to take," Wolfe said. "However, in this office, I always encourage candor. Without it, the kinds of problems I have to grapple with might often go unresolved."

Banks waited close to a half minute before responding, and this time no noises emanated from his throat. "Roger had—has—an unusual personality."

"Please elucidate," Wolfe prodded.

"He was a most difficult person to like. He was opinionated to the point of being insufferable, and he disparaged people, sometimes rather rudely, when they disagreed with his opinions."

"Was that the stimulus for Mr. Wordell to establish the advisory board?"

"I am sure that was at least part of the reason. It had become somewhat widely known within the arts community that Arthur and Roger had begun to have a falling-out. That really should not have surprised anyone, given they both had such strong—and contentious—personalities. The real surprise, at least to me, is that the two got along as well as they did for as long as they did."

"Was there a specific incident that triggered the schism?"

"If there was, I am not aware of it. I must say I was surprised when I got a call from Arthur asking me to be part of that board he was putting together."

"Did you have misgivings about accepting Mr. Wordell's offer?"

"To a degree, yes, I did. On the one hand, I was flattered that he respected my work enough to make the offer, but on the other hand I was wary because of his own rather . . . acerbic personality."

"Did you and Mr. Wordell have differences during the time you served on this board?"

Banks nodded slowly. "To some extent, although probably no more than anyone else who has worked in any capacity with Arthur for a length of time. Say, is that offer of a drink still valid? I seem to have gotten rather dry."

"What will it be?" I asked, going to the bar cart.

"Rye and water on the rocks, if you've got it." We did, and I made the drink, handing it to him.

"Now, where was I?" he asked after a sip. "Oh, yes, my differences with Arthur. I continued to suggest the Guggenheim as the site where his art should go, and he frankly got tired of hearing me on the subject.

"'All right, you have made your point, Henry, don't push it!' he told me and also wrote to me. I also said I thought his collection was somewhat weak on cubist works, which to be honest is a specialty of mine, but he didn't agree there, either. 'I should really drop you from the board! I don't know why in heaven I selected you in the first place,' Arthur said in exasperation when I continued to argue for a greater representation of cubism."

"Did you contemplate resigning after he told you that?"

"Yes, as a matter of fact, I did, Mr. Wolfe. I felt both insulted and demeaned, and I even wrote a letter of resignation, but then I tore it up because I took into account that Arthur was given to angry outbursts, both verbal and on paper. I believed that he often said and wrote things he didn't really mean."

"Did you ever meet with the other two members of this advisory group?" Wolfe asked.

"Yes, three or four times. When we realized that Arthur wasn't ever going to gather all of us together, we felt we should huddle and make sure we had our stories straight, so to speak."

"How did you get along with Miss Richmond and Mr. Sterling?"

"Quite well, on the whole. They both are smart and knowledgeable about a variety of genres. And like me, they were frustrated with Arthur's intractability. As each of us said at one time or another during our meetings, 'Why are we even needed? He doesn't listen to us or care about our opinions.' "

"I assume Mr. Wordell paid each of you to advise him."

"Only what I would term a modest stipend, but I believe that was really fine with all of us. I can't speak for the others, but I would have done it for nothing because of the size and scope of Arthur's collection. What a treasure it is, and I am so glad to have seen at least a portion of it, a portion that is, or was, displayed in his brownstone on the Upper East Side. The rest was in storage."

"Do you know what percentage of Mr. Wordell's art you have seen?"

"I couldn't begin to guess at a percentage, but it is definitely a small minority. What he did display at his home was truly marvelous, and of course he had extensive catalogs of the rest, with photographs."

"It seems a shame the gentleman could not see all his art displayed," Wolfe observed.

"I think that's why he was so anxious to see his collection, or at least the bulk of it, on display in a museum."

"Do you have any idea what will happen to it now?"

Banks shook his head. "I have heard via the grapevine that no will has been found, so I can only assume that either Nadia or Arthur's ex-wife—or both—will be the beneficiaries of the estate, including, of course, all that wonderful art."

"Do you have any further thoughts about Mr. Wordell and his demise?" Wolfe asked.

"I really don't, although I remain firmly convinced that his death was not an accident."

"Why do you believe that?"

"Based on what I have seen of Arthur over these last months, he seemed to be in good health, both physically and mentally. Of course, I suppose he could have slipped off that sill, but from what I learned, he'd been sitting there for years; why would he have fallen when he did?"

"Can you suggest anyone who might have dispatched him to his death?"

Banks swallowed hard. "I have asked myself that question a lot lately, but I can't for the life of me think of anyone who disliked Arthur so much that they would have killed him. Sure, he frustrated a lot of us who were fairly close to him, but as irritating as he could be, that seems to me hardly grounds for murder."

"Very well. I have another engagement, please excuse me," Wolfe said, picking up the telephone. I walked Banks down the hall, and when we reached the front door, he turned to me. "Do you think that Mr. Wolfe has any thoughts about . . . well, about what happened?"

"You have got me there," I said. "My boss is a genius, and most of the time I have no idea what he is thinking." When he tried to continue the conversation, I politely but firmly eased him out and into the night.

CHAPTER 18

When I returned to the office, Wolfe was still at his desk. "Pretty interesting ploy of yours, picking up the phone as if you were actually going to make a telephone call, which of course you never do. That's always been my job around here. Was that phony call nonsense the other engagement you referred to?" I asked.

"No, it is this book," he said, holding up *Aku-Aku* by Thor Heyerdahl. "I had heard enough from Mr. Banks."

"The evening was either funny or sad, depending on your point of view," I told him. "The poor guy comes here trying to pump you for what you've learned about Wordell's death, and he ends up spending almost the whole time getting pumped himself."

"Using your terminology, there was not a great deal to pump out of the man, however."

"True. Do you suspect him? I think that's what he's really worried about, and the reason that he came."

"I am not about to rule him out."

"Good, I didn't much care for him."

"And why not?" Wolfe said.

"I am not entirely sure. Maybe because he seemed awfully nervous. That clearing-of-the-throat business got on my nerves."

"You must work to keep a rein on your nerves, Archie."

"Yeah, right, I will definitely take that under advisement. There are still a couple of people who were close to Wordell that we haven't talked to yet—Mason and the Richmond woman. They have not seen fit to call us."

"That has occurred to me as well."

"Do you want to see them?

"I do. Use your considerable powers of persuasion to get them here. Not together, of course."

"Of course."

Wolfe did not compliment me often, and when he did, it was usually because he wanted something done. So it was that the next morning after breakfast, as I was in the office with coffee, I leafed through the Manhattan white pages and found that both Roger Mason and Faith Richmond were listed, with addresses only a few blocks apart on the Upper West Side.

I started with Mason, who answered after several rings. I identified myself and told him that Wolfe was investigating the Wordell death and would like to talk to him about it.

"And just why would I ever want to speak with Nero Wolfe?" Mason barked. "The police I have talked with appear to believe that Arthur's fall was an accident, and for that matter, so do I."

"Mr. Wolfe is not so sure that is the case, and he thought you might have some insights, having known Mr. Wordell as well as you did."

"Insights, hah! My first insight is that Arthur could turn on someone in the blink of an eye. I do not wish to speak ill of the dead, but in this case, I am happy to make an exception."

"The difficulties that you and Mr. Wordell seem to have encountered were brought up by several of the people Nero Wolfe has spoken to during his ongoing investigation."

"Now just what in the hell is that supposed to mean?"

"Simply that your name was mentioned often during conversations in Mr. Wolfe's office."

"Who brought my name up?" Mason said loudly as I pulled the receiver away from my ear.

"Oh, you would have to ask Mr. Wolfe that yourself. I cannot seem to remember, but I do know that he was extremely interested in the stories that were being told to him."

"Goddammit, I resent this kind of innuendo. It seems like I have a right to know just what is being said about me."

"I totally agree with you, Mr. Mason, which is precisely why I am suggesting that you sit down with Nero Wolfe."

"If what I have heard about your boss is true, he never leaves his home, do I have that right?"

"Yes, you do."

"So I would have to come there to see him, is that what you're telling me?"

"Yes, that's it exactly. But after all, it's no more than a short taxi ride from where you live, twenty minutes at the outside, depending on the time."

"When would he be able to see me?"

"What about tonight, nine o'clock?"

"I . . . yes, I guess so," Mason said in a less than enthusiastic tone. "Would anyone else be present?"

"Just me, and I tend to keep quiet. If Nero Wolfe and I are

business partners, which is open to question, then I am the silent partner."

"All right, I will come tonight," Mason said, still sounding uncertain.

When Wolfe strode into the office later that morning after coddling his orchids, I stopped typing a letter he had dictated to me the day before. "Roger Mason will arrive tonight at nine," I said.

"Satisfactory," he replied, placing an orchid in a vase on his desk, lowering himself into his desk chair, and buzzing for beer. "Do I want to know what tactics you employed to persuade Mr. Mason to present himself here?"

"I don't think so, but I did not threaten him with bodily harm, if that's what you are suggesting."

"I suggest no such thing," Wolfe said as Fritz brought in the beer and the stein and placed them before him.

"What I can say about our conversation is that I believe Mr. Mason will be most anxious to learn what has been said about him by others who have had audiences with you."

"Have you also spoken to Miss Richmond today?"

"No, I exerted all my considerable efforts this morning in delivering the somewhat churlish Mr. Mason to you, but the said lady is next on my list of conquests, so to speak."

"That can wait until after Mr. Mason's visit."

Mason, like all the others involved in this case so far, arrived at the brownstone on time. I wondered as I let him in whether that frown I made note of at the Waldorf dinner was permanently etched on his face. "I hope this is not going to take all night," he grumped as he removed his coat, which I hung on the hall rack.

"Mr. Wolfe does not like to waste anyone's time, most of all his own," I responded while I led Mason down the hall to the office and directed him to the red leather chair. His cheeks were even more hollow than I remembered them from that Waldorf evening, but his disposition seemed to be the same. He settled into the chair and crossed his arms over his chest. "Just where is Wolfe?" he demanded, peering around.

"I am right here, Mr. Mason," he said, walking in and getting seated behind his desk. "Can Mr. Goodwin get you something to drink? I am going to have beer."

Our guest looked at Wolfe with a sour expression. "Beer, now that sounds like a good idea, as long as it's cold. Have you got any more of that stuff handy?"

I went to the kitchen and asked Fritz to bring a beer for our guest in addition to the ones Wolfe had buzzed for. I got back to the office in time to hear Mason saying, ". . . and I am frankly offended that others have chosen to discuss my personal relations during conversations with you."

"Why should you be offended, sir?" Wolfe replied. "As you are aware, I am investigating the death of Arthur Wordell, and in the course of that investigation, I have spoken to a number of individuals, several of whom said less than flattering things about other individuals who knew Mr. Wordell. You were by no means the only individual who was singled out."

Mason took a sip of beer and scowled, which as I suggested earlier seemed to be his normal expression. "Do you believe that Arthur was pushed to his death?" he asked.

"I have not ruled out that possibility. What is your opinion?"

"I happen to think he fell, dammit. I know Arthur was not the most popular of men, but I can't imagine anyone wanting to kill him."

"Had you known Mr. Wordell for a long time?"

"At least ten years. I first met him when I was the director of an art museum up in Connecticut. He had dropped in to see the museum while visiting a man in the same town whom he was buying a Sargent portrait from. I had heard about Arthur and his collection, of course, and I was happy to show him around. We ended up having dinner that night, and I guess you could say that was the beginning of our relationship. I hesitate to call it a friendship, because Arthur was not a man who had what one would term 'friends.'"

"And you communicated regularly after that initial meeting?"

"We did," Mason said. "Arthur seemed to respect my opinions about artists and styles. It got so he would telephone me every few months or so, asking about some painting that he was interested in buying, or some artist whose work he had just discovered. I was surprised that he chose me as an adviser, if you want to call it that. And I also was surprised, to say the least, when he asked me to curate his own collection."

"Did Mr. Wordell make it profitable for you to leave your Connecticut museum to take a position with him?" Wolfe asked.

That brought a dry chuckle from our guest. "I missed New York very much, which as I'm sure you know is far and away the fine arts capital of America," Mason replied. "I suppose you could say I improved financially by going to work for Arthur, but it was the chance to return to Manhattan that really drove my decision."

"How would you describe your relationship with Mr. Wordell at the time of his death?"

"Aha, now we are getting at why you wanted me here—to set me up as a killer. You want a fall guy. Don't try to deny it, Wolfe."

"But I do deny it, Mr. Mason, most emphatically. However, I am curious as to why you think I might be attempting to entrap you."

"All right, let us face the facts," Mason said, spreading his arms. "It was hardly a secret that Arthur and I had our differences. The truth is, I did not always agree with him on matters regarding his collection, and he did not like that. Without so much as a single word to me about what he was doing, he formed that damned advisory board to undercut me. Some advisers—huh! They may be smart people, but they did not have Arthur's best interests at heart."

"Why do you say that?"

"Each of them, all three, accepted Arthur's offer because they thought it would help their respective standings within the arts community. I do not believe any one of them really cared that much about what happened to the Wordell collection."

"But you cared?"

"I most certainly did. I thought his art, or at least the overwhelming portion of it, belonged in the new Guggenheim, and I did not hesitate in telling him my feelings on the subject. A great museum, which I truly believe the Guggenheim will prove to be, merits great art, and some of that great art would have come from Arthur's collection. He was torn in his feelings about the museum, and he did not appreciate my pressing the issue. Now his art may very well end up going to the Guggenheim, depending upon who has the final say regarding its disposition."

"And as you have just said, your position caused friction between you and Mr. Wordell," Wolfe said.

"Yes, but I did not back down."

"Did you ever use threatening words toward him?"

Mason jerked upright and blinked twice. "Why, I . . . suppose it's possible that I might have said something in anger at one time or another."

"If I may refresh your memory," Wolfe said, "you were heard to speak these words to him: 'It would give me great pleasure to strangle you.'"

"I . . . I don't, I can't . . ." Mason muttered, shaking his head and then pounding the desk with his fist. "Just who told you that?" he demanded.

"Do you deny speaking those words to Mr. Wordell?"

"I am not going to say another word. In fact, I am leaving," Mason sputtered as he stood and threw up his arms in anger. "This has been nothing but an attempt to frame me, and I am not going to put up with this kind of treatment." I moved to block his path to the door, but Wolfe shook his head and I stepped aside.

I trailed our unhappy guest down the hall at a discreet distance and watched while he donned his coat and opened the front door. As he stepped outside, he turned and threw me a look over his shoulder that made his feelings toward me crystal clear. No words were needed.

"Well, we did nothing to improve Mr. Mason's state of mind during his visit," I told Wolfe when I got back to the office.

"I will try to avoid concerning myself over his state of mind."

"What do you think of him?"

"The man is unhappy, bitter, and burdened with feelings of inferiority."

"But is he also guilty of murder?"

"Possibly."

"Any other comments about the just completed session with him?"

"None," Wolfe said. "You need to telephone Miss Richmond."

CHAPTER 19

The next morning as I sat in the office with coffee, I got no answer the first two times I tried Faith Richmond's number and finally reached her on my third attempt. When I said that Wolfe wanted to talk to her regarding Wordell's death, I got a snippy reply.

"Really now, just why on earth would I want to talk to your Nero Wolfe? Nothing at all could be gained by such a conversation. I trust that the police will determine what happened to Arthur, and not some private investigator who is just looking to make himself a lot of money as well as getting publicity in the process."

"The police appear to be satisfied that Mr. Wordell's death was an accident. Do you believe that?" I asked.

"I am really not sure what I believe, Mr. Goodwin. But I fail to see how my sitting down with your boss could possibly accomplish anything whatever."

"Perhaps not. But you should know that Nadia is absolutely convinced that her father was murdered. And everyone else who she has suggested we talk to already has had a face-to-face conversation with Mr. Wolfe."

"Oh, now I get it," Faith Richmond said with a dismissive snort. "It's that old 'you are the last holdout' trick. Nice try, but in the first place, I do not believe your boss has talked to all those whom Nadia suggested. And in the second place, even if he has, what have I got to add to what all of them have told him?"

"Number one, Miss Richmond, Nero Wolfe really has had a face-to-face conversation with everyone but you among those who are on Nadia's list, period. Number two, you may have information that you do not realize is important. After all, you did work fairly closely with Mr. Wordell. You may very well be in the possession of some insights that no one else has."

"I doubt that very much, Mr. Goodwin. It seems to me that Nero Wolfe is trying to develop a case where none exists as a way of generating money, as I said before. I have read of some of his past exploits in the newspapers over the years and am aware that he charges high rates. I assume that he has a client. Probably Nadia, right?"

"I'm sorry, but I am not at liberty to comment on that."

"But of course you are not," she harrumphed. "Well, both Mr. Wolfe and his client, whoever that is, will have to do without my contribution, which would be minimal at best."

"That is really too bad, Miss Richmond. It would have been interesting to see whether you could have held your own in a conversation with Mr. Wolfe."

"And what is that supposed to mean?"

"Just that he particularly enjoys verbally sparring with women. He feels he can always get the best of them in a war of words. I am sure that he will be disappointed at your refusal to visit the brownstone. He didn't say so in so many words, but I believe he was really looking forward to having a conversation with you."

"Has your boss already had a session with Zondra Zagreb, or aren't you allowed to say?"

"Yes, they have had a chat."

"And who got the best of that conversation?"

"I'm sorry, I'm not—"

"I know, I know, you are not at liberty to comment," she interrupted in an acid tone. "The fact is, I don't often change my mind, but I also do not believe in being totally rigid. I think I would like to size Nero Wolfe up."

"And why not? He is available tonight at nine."

"At his house, I suppose?"

"Yes, at his house," I said, giving her our address.

"I will be there," she replied. "May I assume you also will be present during the conversation?"

"You may. Do you find that disturbing?"

"Not in the least. In fact, you might find the evening both entertaining and educational."

When Wolfe made his descent from the plant rooms just after eleven that morning, I was able to tell him of my success in persuading Faith Richmond to come to the brownstone.

He raised both eyebrows as he eased into the desk chair built to support his seventh of a ton. "And just what carrot did you dangle before the woman?"

When I reported our conversation to him, he made a growling sound. "Confound it, you need not paint me as some sort of misogynist."

"Look, one of the many reasons you pay me is to get people here who do not want to come. This I have done. And as far as your attitude toward women is concerned, my reaction is to quote the comedian Red Skelton, about whom I'm sure you know nothing whatever: he often says, 'I calls 'em the way I sees 'em.' "

"If you are suggesting that I possess a general antipathy toward the female species, I have told you on more than on occasion that I find women to be astonishing and successful animals. I merely preserve an immunity I developed some years ago by necessity."

I have never known exactly what he means by that and have never bothered to ask him. But I know damned well that with the exception of Lily Rowan, he would rather not have women ever cross the threshold of the brownstone. However, given his line of work, the exceptions he has been forced to make over the years are too numerous to list.

Faith Richmond was a few minutes late in arriving that night, but I gave her some leeway because of a storm in which the rain was coming in sheets horizontally. I opened the front door and welcomed her in, wondering if the thick glasses that freakishly magnify her eyes would faze Wolfe, although I had prepared him for them. I took her umbrella and raincoat, and my smile was returned with a grim expression. An interesting evening lay before us.

I walked Miss Richmond down the hall to the office and directed her to the red leather chair, where she sat on the edge and glared at Wolfe. He set his current book down. "Madam," he said with a slight nod.

"I am not happy to be here," she said by way of introduction.

"Many others have expressed similar feelings," Wolfe responded. "Would you like something to drink? As a bartender, Mr. Goodwin is said to be more than adequate."

"Scotch," she snapped, "assuming that you have a good label. And for heaven's sake, don't ruin it with water; just ice, and not much of that."

I did the honors, handing her a single malt with a couple of cubes, then slid into my desk chair and became the silent and amused onlooker.

"You are investigating the death of Arthur Wordell," Faith Richmond said, leaning forward and making the statement sound like an accusation.

"That is correct," Wolfe replied, considering her, "and I am interested in your thoughts."

"As I told Mr. Goodwin on the telephone, I firmly believe that Arthur fell to his death totally by accident. It was neither suicide nor murder. Period, end of discussion."

"What makes you so sure of your position?"

"Regarding suicide, that is simply laughable. Arthur had far too big an ego to ever do away with himself. And as for murder—really, who would want to kill him? He was cantankerous, there is no question about that, and hard to get along with. But if everyone who possessed those traits got murdered, the mortuaries in this town couldn't keep up with the business."

"Your point is well taken," Wolfe said. "How would you describe your relationship with Mr. Wordell?"

"Ah, here it comes as I expected," Faith said, holding her glass up as if in a mock toast. "The private detective seeks to find some reason why I might have wanted to do violence to Arthur."

"Madam, I fear you have read more into my question than was intended," Wolfe told her calmly. "Is it accurate to describe yourself as a friend of the deceased gentleman?"

It was clear to me that Faith Richmond was on her guard. "I am not sure that Arthur ever possessed what you might term to be friends. Acquaintances, well, yes . . . but friends? I really don't believe so."

"However, Mr. Wordell must have held you in high esteem to have named you to his advisory board."

"I am not so sure of that. It is true, of course, that he had a falling-out with Roger Mason over I don't know what, and I think maybe he brought the three of us on board at least in part to irritate or to spite Roger."

"Was Mr. Wordell inclined toward fits of pique?"

"That I can't say for sure, as I really did not know him all that well. But as I mentioned moments ago, he could be irascible, testy, cranky—feel free to add your own synonyms."

"In your role on the advisory board, did you find him to be difficult?"

Faith took a sip of her scotch and set the glass down carefully on the small table next to her chair. "He was invariably critical of my suggestions, as well as those of the others on the board."

"For example?"

"I had strongly advised him to increase the amount of his twentieth-century art, which is where I felt that his collection was at its weakest. But he merely brushed that suggestion aside.

" 'That has been your specialty as a writer,' Arthur told me in a condescending tone, 'so of course you would want to see more of your favorites represented. I should have been prepared for that from you.' I was somewhat put out, but as I said, he was just as dismissive of suggestions by the other members of the board, sometimes even more so."

"Did you meet often as a group?"

"Hah—the answer to that is never! He would telephone or see each of us separately and ask our opinions, which he often disagreed with. We were really a board in name only, although the three of us did sit down on several occasions to . . . well, to complain and to wonder aloud as to why he even wanted or needed our advice."

"When each of you met separately with Mr. Wordell, where did these sessions take place?"

"Sometimes in that depressing old office in Midtown, but more often at his home on the Upper East Side."

"When you visited 'that depressing old office,' did Mr. Wordell ever perch on the windowsill?"

"That terrible windowsill! Yes, one time when I went to see him, he was sitting on it and I must have looked horrified—I am sure that I did—because he hopped down and we talked with him sitting at his desk with me across from him."

"How did you come to meet Mr. Wordell?"

"It has been more than twenty years ago now, back when I was a graduate student in fine arts at Columbia. I was writing a paper on collectors, and I called Arthur, who had already begun to make a name for himself in amassing art. I asked if I could interview him. At first, he was reticent, but he gave in to what probably was my pleading tone, and we met at that town house of his on the Upper East Side.

"He seemed to like the questions I asked him, and he told me so. I must have made a greater impression than I realized at the time, because on two or three occasions over the years after I became an author, he called me and asked my opinion about works he was thinking of buying. And then, more recently, out of the clear blue sky, he called and asked if I would be on his advisory board."

"Did you immediately accept?" Wolfe asked.

She nodded. "I was quite flattered, little knowing at the time that the board would not have any real advisory function, and that, as I said before, Arthur's real reason for setting up the triumvirate may well have been mainly to spite Roger Mason."

"How would you describe your personal feelings for Mr. Wordell?"

She looked askance at Wolfe. "I think I've already defined that. What have I left out?"

"Precisely how you felt about him."

"What are you suggesting," Faith Richmond said, inhaling and letting out the air with a whoosh.

"I am suggesting you grew to have an interest in Mr. Wordell that went beyond your business association."

"Well, if that isn't just typical!" she flared, putting her hands on her hips in a defiant pose. "Whenever a woman has any type of a relationship with a man, it is invariably assumed—always by other men like you, of course—that she is somehow romantically involved with the individual, or desires to be."

"And you categorically state that was not true?"

"What would make you think otherwise?"

"The fact that such has been suggested."

"And just who did the suggesting?" she asked.

"Let us not get ahead of ourselves," Wolfe said, holding up a hand.

"What man suggested that?"

"We should not assume too much."

"So . . . it was a woman? Oh, of course—probably his estranged wife, that, that . . . Well, never mind what I think of her, it's not worth discussing. But if you believe what she tells you, I am afraid that you are beyond help."

"You may be correct about that, madam, but I will do my best to soldier on. Do you have anything further to say about relations between you and Mr. Wordell?"

She cut loose with a laugh, which surprised me. "I feel that anything I say will be akin to that poor soul who was asked in court, 'When did you stop beating your wife?' No answer I could give to your question would satisfy you, although frankly, I see no need whatever to satisfy you. You have turned out to be pretty much as I expected. Good evening."

I will give Faith Richmond credit. She rose gracefully, executed a nice turn, and swept out of the office like an actress leaving the stage. I almost felt like clapping at the style of her exit, not the first by a woman in this case. I went down the hall a few paces behind her and got to the rack in time to help her on with her raincoat and pull her umbrella out of the stand.

"I do not know how you can stand to work for that man," she said, fixing me with those magnified eyes, "unless you are like him. I do so hope you are able to sleep nights, Mr. Goodwin."

I started to respond that I always sleep very well—a full eight hours—but she was already out the door and down the front steps. She seemed the type who would be able to hail a cab without the help of me or any other man, so I locked the door behind her.

"An interesting evening," I told Wolfe when I got back to the office.

"Not the adjective I would have chosen, but no matter," he replied. "Honor and respect be to the woman who defends herself fiercely."

"Very nice. Is that Shakespeare? Or the Bible?"

"Neither, it is me. Miss Richmond is a formidable creature."

"Not the adjective I would have chosen, but no matter," I said, aping his comment. "Do I have instructions before I retire?"

"Not at the moment," Wolfe said, turning to a *New York Times* Sunday crossword puzzle, which he always did using a pen.

CHAPTER 20

For the next two days, no instructions on the Wordell case were forthcoming from Wolfe, and I began to worry that he was having one of his relapses. These come periodically and they are caused by any number of factors, among them his frustration at having to work hard on a case, although I saw no examples of mental strain on this particular project.

A few words about Wolfean relapses: These can last anywhere from a day to several weeks. Sometimes he takes to his bed, refusing to see anyone except Fritz, who brings him his meals. During a relapse, the daily schedule is thrown into disarray, with Wolfe forgoing his twice daily visits to the orchids. He also goes on eating binges, such as the time he ate half a sheep in two days, its various parts cooked twenty different ways. And there was the episode where he devoured a ten-pound goose in four hours.

Just when I began to think we had entered relapse mode, help came from an unlikely and oddly welcome source. Wolfe had just descended from the plant rooms one morning when the doorbell rang. I went to answer it and through the one-way glass in the front door saw the recognizable and substantial silhouette of Inspector Cramer of Homicide.

"What a nice surprise," I said, swinging the door open. "We were not expecting you."

"Humbug," he growled, stomping in and marching past me as though I were invisible. I followed him to the office and arrived just as he dropped into the red leather chair and whipped out a cigar, which he did not torch. "Well?" he snorted at Wolfe.

"Well, indeed, sir. What brings you today?"

"What else? It's this damned Wordell business. Ever since the commissioner read that you were investigating the man's death, he's been all over me to reopen our investigation."

"And have you?"

"Not yet, but you had better believe that I'm feeling the heat from upstairs. Where do you stand right now, or is that confidential?"

"I have been talking to people who knew and worked with Mr. Wordell, as has Archie."

"And . . . ?"

"And, at the moment, we are taking a step back and considering the situation."

"But you still believe Wordell was pushed to his death?"

"I do, unequivocally."

"Why?"

"You are a man of few words today, sir. I can only tell you that from what I have learned about Mr. Wordell from his relatives and acquaintances, I find it incomprehensible that he could have taken his own life or slipped from his perch. That leaves only one alternative."

"So everybody who knows him thinks he was killed?"

"I did not say that. There are some in his circle who believe he was the victim of an accident, but they are in a minority."

Cramer gnawed on his unlit stogie. "I need to make sure of myself here, or I—and the entire Homicide Squad—will have egg on our collective faces if it turns out to be an accident or a suicide."

"I sympathize with your position, but I do not see that I can be of substantive aid. I am continuing to feel my way. Archie, do you have anything to add?" he asked, turning to me.

"No, sir. If you are still in the dark, I am even farther from knowing just who killed Wordell, and why."

"There you are," Wolfe told Cramer.

"Well, one thing I do know is that the daughter, Nadia, is absolutely convinced that her father was killed. I've talked to her and now it looks like I will be talking to her again. Then there is the widow, or estranged wife, or whatever you choose to call that woman. She has been to see me twice, which was no picnic, and she is as determined as the daughter to believe that this was a killing. I assume that you've spent time with her."

"I have."

"Lots of fun, isn't she?" Cramer snarled. "I don't suppose you're going to tell me who your client is. I know damned well that you wouldn't undertake this investigation—or any investigation, for that matter—as pro bono work."

"No, I am not going to divulge my client's identity and—another no—I do not as a matter of course engage in what you refer to as pro bono work."

"It looks like we will be plowing old ground—that is, talking to most of the same people you have already taken through the paces. And they will likely be grumpy because they will be forced to repeat what they have already told you. As usual, I will come away from here empty-handed, but then I shouldn't be surprised. Leopards do not change their spots," Cramer said, rising, putting his battered fedora on, throwing his cigar at the wastebasket, and missing it as usual. He walked out of the office without another word and lumbered down the hall to the door.

"So how does it feel to be a leopard?" I asked Wolfe when I got back to the office after bolting the door behind Cramer.

"The inspector has only a few adages in his repertoire, Archie. Do not be too hard on him."

"By the way, that was really damned cute of you, asking me if I had anything to add regarding the investigation. I'm curious as to how you thought I'd respond?"

"Essentially as you did."

"Yeah, well, I'm sure Cramer was not impressed. So just where do we go from here?"

"Mr. Cramer finds himself in a box of sorts. I believe he still does not feel Mr. Wordell was pushed to his death, but he is being forced by circumstances to conduct a murder investigation."

I grinned. "The circumstances in this case being *you*. Are you thinking that he won't put his heart into the project?"

"Knowing the inspector, I believe he will make a valiant effort, but we have a head start on him, not that we are in competition. Please call Mr. Cohen; I would like to speak to him."

Lon picked up before the first ring had stopped and barked his name. I barked mine right back at him. "And here I thought that you had forgotten all about me," he snapped, trying without success to sound hurt.

"How could we ever forget about you, Mr. Deadline-Every-Minute? Nero Wolfe is on the wire and would like to swap words with you."

"Hello, Mr. Cohen. Has your army of news gatherers found anything new of interest regarding the death of Arthur Wordell?"

"I should be the one asking that of you. But from this end, the answer is no, although we have got one of our best men still doing a bit of poking around."

"I thought there might be some rumors worth pursuing, although I know you insist the *Gazette* does not deal in rumor, or perhaps you would prefer I use the term hearsay."

That brought a dry chuckle from Lon. "Off the record, we do occasionally look into a rumor on the slim chance that it may have some substance. But nothing has surfaced on the Wordell case for days. Even our sleazy competitor's Keyhole Peeper column has been silent on the subject. And the police also don't seem interested, for that matter."

"That may soon change," Wolfe said.

"Oh. And just what do you know that I don't?"

"I suggest you call Inspector Cramer and inquire as to whether the department has decided Mr. Wordell's death may be a homicide."

"Hmm. Does this mean that I owe you one?"

"Let your conscience be your guide, Mr. Cohen."

"Well, I will be damned. Put me down as grateful."

"I will have Archie make note of that in our Cohen file."

"No doubt it is a thick one."

"A fair statement, sir," Wolfe said as he cradled his receiver. I stayed on the line, asking Lon what he would ever do if we weren't supplying him and the *Gazette* with key pieces of information.

"It's funny, hotshot gumshoe, that you never seem to raise that subject when we are the ones who are feeding you information."

"No comment," I replied and we rang off. "Well, you threw Lon a bone," I told Wolfe. "Do you think that we'll get anything from him in return?"

"We can't be sure, but it will cost us nothing to share some information with an ally."

"Should we be reporting to Nadia Wordell? After all, she *is* our client."

"What can we report?" Wolfe asked, turning his hands palms up. "Let her call us if she feels the need for information, although at the moment she would receive a paucity of it at this end."

"Give me some instructions. I find myself getting antsy, and when I get antsy, I get crabby."

"I never would have guessed it."

"Sarcasm has never been one of your strong suits," I told him. "To repeat . . . instructions?"

"I believe Miss Wordell and her father have a lawyer in common, as she has suggested."

"I don't know who that is, but I can find out."

"Please do."

"And then what?'

"I would like to meet with the individual, or individuals."

"When?"

"Preferably tonight." Just another routine request from my boss.

CHAPTER 21

I called Nadia, who sounded like she was glad to hear from me. "Before you get too excited at the sound of my voice, let me tell you that we have no news and are still casting about. You have a lawyer, I believe?"

"Yes, Charles Applegate."

"And if I remember correctly, he also represented your father?"

"Oh, yes, Daddy thought we should have the same individual. 'Your interests and mine are identical,' he told me. Mr. Applegate has done a good job for us, Archie."

"Nero Wolfe would like to talk to him. Can you telephone the gentleman and tell him to expect a call from me?"

"Yes, yes, I can."

"And when you do, please tell him to be totally candid with us. Make sure he knows that you are Mr. Wolfe's client and that he has your best interests at heart, which you know to be true."

"I will, Archie."

Nadia called me a half hour later to say that Applegate was awaiting our call, and she gave me his number. I dialed and got a sweet-sounding woman who informed me I had reached "the office of Applegate & Simmons."

I identified myself as Archie Goodwin from Nero Wolfe's office and was immediately put through to Charles Applegate.

"That was fast," he said in an amiable tone. "I have barely hung up from talking to Nadia, Mr. Goodwin. I understand from her that Nero Wolfe wishes to speak to me."

"Yes, sir, tonight, if you are free. Preferably nine o'clock."

"Tonight? My, that is short notice. I know just enough about the famous Mr. Wolfe to realize that he almost never leaves his home, is that correct?"

"It is."

A protracted sigh came through the line. "All right, anything for dear Nadia, who has been through a great deal recently. Give me the address."

I reported my progress to Wolfe, who was unimpressed. That's the trouble with my consistently delivering on his requests. He thinks I can make rabbits jump out of hats, so to speak. He ought to try working the telephone himself sometime, as if that would ever happen. But then, as I've said before, it is all part of what he pays me for.

It was no surprise that Charles Applegate rang our doorbell at three minutes to nine. He had sounded like the model of dependability on the phone. "Please come in," I said.

"And you would be Archie Goodwin, of course," he replied. "Nadia speaks highly of you."

Applegate was probably in his early- to mid-sixties, ruddy cheeked, slightly overweight, and well tailored in a three-piece blue pinstripe. And yes, he was carrying a briefcase.

I hung his raincoat on the rack and led the way down the hall to the office, where as if by instinct he made for the red leather chair. "Good evening, sir," Nero Wolfe said, putting down his current book.

"Mr. Wolfe," Applegate said, nodding and settling into the chair. Maybe Nadia had told him of his host's aversion to shaking hands. "Miss Wordell made it clear to me that I should consider you a friend. She has placed a great deal of trust in you and in your abilities, which I have of course read about."

"Duly noted," Wolfe said. "Would you like something to drink? As you see, I am having beer."

"Scotch would be good," Applegate said, eyeing the drink cart against the wall. I hastened to fill the order.

Once the lawyer had been served, he turned to Wolfe. "What can I do to help with your investigation?"

"I am not sure," Wolfe replied. "Perhaps you are able to shed some light on Arthur Wordell's refusal to draw up a will."

Applegate looked down at his lap and then up again. "I consider that to be one of my signal failures," he said. "I had tried for years, literally for years, to get Arthur to put his house in order. But he was an exceedingly stubborn individual, as you probably have learned."

"I have, from several sources," Wolfe said.

"Arthur seemed to think that he was going to live forever," the attorney said. "Both Nadia and I brought up the subject numerous times, and he just dug in his heels. He would say things like, 'I will draw up a will when I am good and ready, and the time has not yet come.' That attitude probably was exacerbated by the fact that his health was excellent. I really felt he was going to live well into his nineties, and he may very well have, if . . ."

"Was there any sound legal reason why Mr. Wordell would have been better off without a will?" Wolfe asked.

"None whatever! As it is, there's some confusion as to the rights of Arthur's . . . his wife."

"How is that confusion likely to manifest itself?"

"I am not entirely sure. I haven't been in touch with Alexis's counselor, who for whatever reason chooses not to return my calls."

"Which suggests that the woman is seeking a major portion of the estate?"

"I don't know, Mr. Wolfe," Applegate said, shrugging. "Nadia urged me to be completely candid with you. I can say that I have always been suspicious about Alexis's refusal to grant Arthur a divorce. She claimed it had to do with her Catholicism."

"I gather you do not believe that."

"I hesitate to criticize anyone's stance on religious grounds, but her position had puzzled me, especially as Arthur was extremely generous with her when they separated."

"Are you suggesting she felt by not divorcing Mr. Wordell, she would receive a larger portion of his estate at his death?"

Applegate allowed himself a chuckle. "I suppose that is what I am suggesting. By all accounts, the woman had plenty to live on, both from her first husband and from all that Arthur had already settled upon her."

"Did she have her eyes on the Wordell art collection?" Wolfe asked.

"That is what Nadia believes, and she has no compunctions in my sharing her belief with you."

"I have been told by what I consider to be reliable sources that Mr. Wordell was in good health at the time of his death."

"That is also my understanding," Applegate said, "which might suggest Alexis would figure to wait a long time to receive any more of Arthur's estate, including perhaps his art."

"Do you believe Alexis Wordell to be capable of murder?" Wolfe asked.

"Whoa!" Applegate said, throwing up both hands. "Nadia wanted me to be candid, but I am not willing to go that far, even in a confidential conversation, which I believe this to be. Mr. Wolfe, I don't know enough about Arthur's death to even hazard an opinion as to whether he fell by accident or was pushed. Either way, it was a terrible tragedy. I know that many people did not find Arthur to be friendly, but to say someone wanted him dead—I simply have trouble believing that. But then, I am a poor one to judge. I live in a legal world, one that mostly involves estate work, not a violent one like you and Mr. Goodwin have experienced in your line of work."

"Sometimes, I wonder how different our worlds are from each other," Wolfe said.

"You raise an interesting point," Applegate said. "I do not deal in violence, per se, although in many of my cases, I can sense violence in a client that is bubbling up just beneath the surface. This would be a good subject for another time," the attorney added, smiling. "Do you have further need of me?"

"I do not believe so, sir," Wolfe said. "Thank you for your time."

CHAPTER 22

"Well, what did you think of Nadia's counselor?" I asked Wolfe after I had seen Applegate out.

"As you know, my opinion of lawyers does not put them in the front rank of professions. However, I feel Mr. Applegate is well worthy of Nadia Wordell's trust."

"I agree. He seems to be an all-right guy. Did you draw any conclusions from his visit?"

"Nothing of significance, other than his low opinion of Mrs. Wordell, which hardly places him in a minority."

"So where do we go from here?"

"Ah, yes, as a man of action, you are anxious to do something. We just can't have you sitting around here like—what was it you once called yourself—a time bomb?"

"Yes, sir, I am liable to go off at any time."

"We cannot have that. You have not yet been to Mr. Wordell's residence on the Upper East Side. I believe a visit is in order."

"To what end, if I may ask?"

"Have his daughter show you around the abode. Something may present itself to you."

Ah, so as I suspected we were truly and totally adrift. Wolfe wanted it to seem as if we were taking action, so he was sending me out on what seemed like a pointless mission. But mine was not to reason why . . .

I called Nadia the next day and asked if I could see her father's brownstone. "I will be happy to let you in, Archie. Do you have any idea what you might be expecting to find there?"

"Honestly, I do not, but I would like to see your father's files and go through them."

"Have you ever read Charles Dickens?" she asked.

"Years ago, as a kid in high school, I got assigned one or two of his stories, but I'm afraid I don't remember much, if anything about them. That was a long time ago. Why do you ask?"

"In *David Copperfield*, there is a wonderful and eccentric character named Wilkins Micawber, an eternal optimist who despite his misfortunes throughout the story repeatedly insists that 'something will turn up.' "

"Did something ever turn up—for this Micawber guy, I mean?"

"Yes, it did, in Australia, of all places. But there I go, reliving my student life as an English major. Sorry."

"Nothing to be sorry about," I told her. "I always like to learn new things. Maybe now I'll read *David Copperfield* to find out what happened to Micawber. And maybe something will also turn up in your father's files."

"When would you like to see the brownstone?" Nadia said.

"I can be there almost anytime."

"As soon as possible, given your schedule."

"I have a lunch engagement, but I don't expect it to run long. What if I meet you at Daddy's at two thirty?"

"That works well for me," I said, getting the address from Nadia.

CHAPTER 23

I climbed out of a cab at the Wordell address in the Yorkville neighborhood at 2:25. Arthur's three-story brick home, along with several of its similar-size neighbors, was in a stretch in the East Eighties that had yet to undergo the invasion of new, far taller, and uninspired buildings that other nearby blocks had experienced in the building boom of recent years.

I had just started up the steps when the elaborate wooden door swung open to reveal a smiling Nadia. "Our timing is just perfect, Archie," she said. "I got here less than five minutes ago."

I stepped across the threshold and found myself in a six-sided paneled foyer with a vaulted ceiling dominated by a crystal chandelier that had more small lightbulbs than I cared to count. "I wouldn't want to dust that thing," I said, bringing a laugh from my hostess.

"Leave it to a man to come up with a comment like that. I really don't have any idea who is going to dust it now, as I have let the butler, the cook, and the housekeeper go. I have also gotten a real estate agent lined up, and I plan to put this place on the market soon so somebody else can worry about the chandelier and everything else in this place.

"Although I have just gotten some inkling that Alexis may want it for herself. Since Daddy deeded it to me, she'll have to come to me, and I just might drive a hard bargain. Come on in and I'll give you the full tour."

The first floor included a sitting room facing the street—Nadia referred to it as a parlor—along with a dining room that seated eight, a kitchen that was just about the size of Wolfe's, and a large pantry that included a floor-to-ceiling wine rack with most of its spaces filled.

On the second floor were Wordell's office, a library with built-in bookcases dominating two walls, and a guest bedroom with an attached bath. The top floor was composed of three bedrooms, including the master suite. None of the staff had ever lived in, Nadia said.

"Daddy really rattled around in here, with far more space than he needed, but he always seemed to like it that way," Nadia said as we went back down to his office, where I planned to start my snooping.

"I had suggested he take a full floor in one of those pricey Park Avenue co-ops so that he wouldn't have to climb stairs," she continued, "but he dismissed that idea with a grumble and he also refused to put in an elevator here.

" 'I like the stairs, dammit,' he told me. 'It's good to keep the old heart pumping by going up and down. The day will come when I can't do that, but it's not here yet, not by a long shot.' "

"Well, judging by my one meeting with him, your father seemed to have kept in awfully good shape, and he didn't seem to have an extra pound on him."

"Yes, he was always proud of his good health," Nadia said, suddenly sober. "I think he could have lived another . . ." Her voice trailed off, and I did not attempt to help her finish the sentence.

When she recovered her composure, she said, "Feel free to look at everything here, whether it's in the office, the library, or anywhere else. I've merged the files from the Midtown space with those here. And I have gone through them, but only in the most cursory manner. I am afraid that I would not have made a good detective."

"I often think that about myself," I told her.

"I don't believe it for a minute, Archie Goodwin," she said with a smile, punching me playfully in the arm. "Where would you like to start?"

"I think I will tackle those files first."

"That is just fine by me. I will be across the hall in the library. I need to figure out how to dispose of all the books. Large numbers of the volumes, no surprise, are tomes, many of them quite large, about art and artists. Some are absolutely beautiful with all their color plates on glossy paper. I am thinking about which of the museums they might go to."

"You said before that your father gave this place to you, and that you think Alexis might want to buy it. Has she said anything to you?"

"No, and she would not have, as we really don't communicate. But some months ago, Daddy told me that Alexis had always shown an interest in having this as her home."

"Didn't she and your father live here before their separation?"

"No, they were over at a big old place on Central Park West. It was only after they split up that Daddy bought this. But I do remember that Alexis came here once for a meeting with Daddy, probably to iron out part of the settlement, and it was clear to me that she was impressed."

"I gather that you have no desire to live here."

"I really don't, Archie. I'm very comfortable where I am. This is just far too much house for me."

"But not for your dear stepmother, Alexis, I take it?"

Nadia responded with a full-throated laugh, which was good to hear. "I enjoy your sense of humor, Archie," she said. "You cheer me up. And as I told you earlier, if 'dear' Alexis really wants this house badly, as I suspect, she will pay my asking price—and not a red cent less."

"I'm glad to hear that; I like your style," I told her. While she headed across the hall to the library, I went into the office and looked it over. *Why in heaven's name*, I thought, *did Wordell want to spend time in that Midtown dump when he could have been here with all its comforts?*

If I were ever to design an office just for myself, Wordell's would come very close to the ideal: one window that looked out onto the tree-lined street, light-colored walls that made the room seem larger than it was, a desk similar to Wolfe's, a chair that was comfortable—I tested it—a sofa, and two guest chairs. Three lamps were nicely spread around the room, plus one on the desk. And, oh, yes, the three-drawer file cabinet, which is in large part why I happened to be here.

I eventually pulled out all the manila file folders, many of which I ignored, such as those dealing with American museums, European museums, Asian museums, and art restorers, along with the dozens of folders devoted to auctions, at which Arthur Wordell was said to have often outbid anyone who dared to stand in his way for a specific piece of art.

I did look through a few of the auction folders and was interested to note that the collector kept carbons of all his correspondence, along with notes he made, never imagining that they would ever be seen by others. Here are some handwritten notes from the auction files, which say a great deal about their writer:

Idiot from California thought that he could beat me to a Manet, but I crushed him and sent him running from the room. He never returned.

The poor woman with her diamond rings and pearls never had a chance at the Toulouse-Lautrec poster. She thought that she could outbid me, hah!

That arrogant Bostonian actually was sure he was going to take away a Winslow Homer seascape. After I was through, he didn't know what hit him. You might say I blew him out of the water, so to speak!!!

Okay, so maybe Wordell's comedy routine needed work.

I was far more interested in those files dealing with the people closest to the collector. And there was a folder for every one of them: Emory Sterling, Boyd Tatum, Henry Banks, Roger Mason, Faith Richmond, Zondra Zagreb, and of course, Alexis Evans Farrell Wordell.

It was going to take longer than I had originally thought to give these files the attention that I felt they deserved, so I telephoned Fritz and told him not to expect me home for dinner. Then I waded into the folders of those individuals who knew Wordell well.

Here are some selected carbon examples of the neatly typed correspondence from the collector, which I can only assume were done by Mabel Courtney, as she did not put her initials at the bottom of the sheet as I do when typing Wolfe's letters:

Dear Miss Richmond:

At the risk of repeating myself, I have no interest whatever in increasing my holdings of twentieth-century art, and I wish you would kindly refrain from bringing up the subject again. I am sick and tired of hearing about it.

Yrs. Truly,

Dear Mr. Tatum:

You persist in trying to get me to agree to be the subject of a biography related to my art collecting. Please do not raise the subject with me again, as I am not under any circumstances going to budge from my position. I am not interested, and if you are trying to irritate me, I assure you that you are succeeding!

Yrs. Angrily,

Dear Mr. Sterling:

I am delighted that you have given up on your idea of having an article on me and my collection in your Art & Artists publication. I told you from the beginning that I would not cooperate with your editors in the writing of such an article, and I am disappointed that you chose to push ahead as long as you did.

Yrs.

Dear Roger:

I regret that you are unhappy with my decision to form an advisory board to provide me with counsel about my collection, but I greatly feel the need for such a group. If you seek a reason, I can only say I feel you have come to look on my collection as your own personal possession. I, and only I, will make the final decisions as to its disposition.

Sincerely,

Dear Zondra,

As much as I like you, and I assure you that is the case, I feel it is time for both of us to come to the realization that our

relationship is an unrealistic one and should be ended. I know you will understand this, being the perceptive individual that you are.
  My best,

That "Dear Jane" letter explained Mabel Courtney's reluctance to discuss Zondra Zagreb with me in any detail when I visited her. She was being loyal to her late employer, and she saw no need to tell me anything whatever about his relationship with Miss Zagreb, an attitude that I respect. I continued combing the files, turning to the one for Henry Banks.

Dear Mr. Banks,
  I have grown tired of your carping about how my collection "must" go to the Guggenheim. I, and I alone, will decide where my art will reside. And another thing: Kindly stop prattling on about cubist art. I have all of it that I want. I continue to wonder why I ever asked you to be on my board.
  Yrs.

So what Banks had told Wolfe and me about his rocky relationship with Wordell certainly was borne out in this letter, some of it word for word. Now for the file folder containing correspondence between Wordell and his wife. After going through the stack of their letters to each other, many of them barely civil, I chose this last missive, dated three weeks ago, to take home, along with the ones above.

Dear Alexis,
  It would seem that we find ourselves at an impasse. You continue to whine to me about your wanting to get some of my art, and I continue to tell you the generous amounts I have settled upon you are more than sufficient to allow you to live like a

queen, along with everything that you received from your first wealthy husband. I find your secrecy interesting in regards to the amount that man left you. I shall say—or write—no more on the subject. Any further correspondence should be directed to my lawyer, whose address you have.

With finality,

I gathered the letters I would take to Wolfe and found Nadia across the hall in the library, where she was sitting cross-legged on the floor among stacks of art books piled next to her. "Well, did you find anything of interest, Archie?"

"Probably not, although I will leave it to Nero Wolfe to decide if he sees something that leaps off the page," I said, holding out the stack of carbons. "Do you want to look at what I'm taking with me?"

"That's not really necessary," she replied. "Maybe some of what you have will help."

"I must say that your father was not one to hide his feelings, based on what I have read."

That brought another laugh from Nadia. If nothing else, I do seem to be able to cheer the young woman up.

"I looked through a lot of those letters of his myself, Archie, and if I were to choose one word to describe their tone, it would be *acerbic.*"

"That is a word that my boss has used on any number of occasions," I told her.

"Then I guess that puts me in good company. I haven't been around Mr. Wolfe very much, but just enough to know that he seems to be a real stickler for grammar and usage."

"You had better believe it. I can't tell you the number of times he has chided me for some word or another that I have misused. I've gotten better over the years, but I still rile him up sometimes, and I suppose with good reason."

"You poor baby."

"Yeah, it's a rough life, let me tell you."

"I'll just bet. Well, you always have Lily Rowan to comfort you. I have to believe a lot of men must envy you that relationship."

"True, although even Lily gets after me sometimes if I stub my toe over a certain word."

"I'm sure that you are able to put up with that."

"I am," I told Nadia, thanking her and stepping out onto the street in search of a cab.

CHAPTER 24

In the southbound cab, I looked at my watch, surprised to learn how long I had been at Arthur Wordell's home. Back at the brownstone, I let myself in with my key and went straight to the office, where Wolfe sat at his desk with coffee.

"You missed dinner," he said, looking up from his book and stating the obvious. "But Fritz has saved you a plate of the duck Mondor."

"Bless that man. I have spent hours going through reams of correspondence to and from Arthur Wordell, and I have concluded that if any of those people who were close to him could be termed friends, I would hate to see how he would have treated his enemies."

"It is clear he was not a man who encouraged or sought close relationships."

"I will second that. I have brought back some samples of his correspondence. I am not sure if any of this stuff helps us, but I felt you should see why at least some of his associates might not spend a lot of time in mourning his passing." I handed the stack of carbons to Wolfe, who flipped through them once, and then studied them a second time more slowly.

"Nothing in here astonishes me," he said, "based on what has been said about the man in this office. Are you surprised?"

"No, and I have got the added advantage, if you want to call it that, of having met him, albeit briefly at that dinner. But it did not take me long at all to see what a curmudgeon he was."

"I have not heard that word in your conversation before," Wolfe said. "But from what I have learned of Mr. Wordell, you are using it correctly if you mean to describe him as ill-tempered, crusty, and generally disagreeable."

"Bingo on all three. But so what?"

"So what indeed? Do any of these letters prove anything about him that we did not already know?"

I shook my head. "It seems like I wasted my time wading through all those damned files."

"Not necessarily," Wolfe said, closing his eyes. I hoped he would start doing that exercise where his lips pushed in and out, in and out, indicating he was in the process of solving the problem. I had seen this happen countless times in the past.

But this was not to be one of those occasions. He opened his eyes after several seconds and blinked. "Will Mr. Cohen be in his office at this time?" he asked.

"I suppose so," I said. "The *Gazette* still has one or two more editions to put out today. Should I call him?"

His answer was a dip of the chin, so I dialed a familiar number and Wolfe picked up his instrument. "Yeah, Cohen here," came the clipped reply.

"You really need to work on your telephone etiquette," I told him. "Someone wishes to speak with you."

"Good afternoon, Mr. Cohen," Nero Wolfe said. "Has anything new arisen regarding Arthur Wordell's death?"

"Not a whisper. We do know, thanks to you, that the police are now at least considering that he might have been pushed to his death. But our man, whom I mentioned before and who has been bulldogging the story, hasn't been able to get five words out of Cramer or anyone else in Homicide on the subject."

Wolfe thanked Lon and hung up, turning to me. "Would Mr. Cramer likely be available now?"

"I suppose so, unless he's out chasing down some murderer. But he usually leaves that to his underlings. After all, rank does have its privileges—along with its headaches, of course."

"Try him at work, and if he's not there, at home."

I had no idea where Wolfe was going with this, but that was often the case. I dialed Cramer at Homicide, and he answered his own phone, which also is usually the case with Lon Cohen.

"Nero Wolfe is on the line," I told him.

"Pardon my bothering you, sir. I am curious as to whether you have discovered anything pertinent to the death of Arthur Wordell."

"Nero Wolfe, asking *me* for information?" Cramer replied. "What is the world coming to? But in answer to your question, we have gotten nowhere. Since we are on the subject, do you have anything to tell me?"

"No, sir, sadly, I do not." Cramer made an exhaling sound and the conversation ended.

Wolfe leaned back in his chair and pressed his palms over his eyes. At that moment, I realized something I had rarely if ever experienced: he was stymied, totally and unequivocally. Or was he? His next sentence stunned me.

"I want to see everyone here. That includes: Messrs. Sterling, Tatum, Banks, and Mason; Mrs. Wordell; and Misses Zagreb, Richmond, and Wordell."

"Swell, a party of eight, enough for two tables of bridge. And just when would you like this to happen?"

"Preferably this week," Wolfe said. "Today is Tuesday, which gives you four nights from which to choose. Obviously, I would like this gathering to occur as soon as possible. Let us try for Thursday, which seems a realistic goal."

"Obviously," I said, meaning my playing in the poker game was off for this week. "Is there anything specific you would like me to relay to any or all of these individuals?"

"That I plan to discuss the death of Arthur Wordell."

"And what happens if I am unable to get every one of this octet to make an appearance?"

"I trust you will use your intelligence guided by experience to persuade them to attend," Wolfe said, mouthing a line he had thrown my way countless times in the past.

I had my assignment, which I did not relish. But I had been put in this position before, and I likely would be many more times in the future. The best way to begin, based on that past experience Wolfe referred to, was to nail down the easy ones first.

I started calling after breakfast Wednesday morning. I figured the most likely one I could persuade to attend was Emory Sterling, and I was correct.

"Tomorrow night? Yes, I can be there," he said. "Is there anything that you are able to share with me about the program?"

"No, because in all honesty, nothing has been shared with me. Mr. Wolfe has set the meeting for nine o'clock." Sterling said he would make it, so I moved on to Zondra Zagreb.

"Thursday at nine, Archie? Well . . . yes, I guess I would be able to come, despite the way Mr. Wolfe treated me when I was there before. Just what should I be expecting from this gathering?"

"I am really not sure, given that my boss likes to set the agenda, and he does not always take me into his confidence. But as I said, the subject will be Mr. Wordell's death."

"And the person who was responsible for it?"

"That I can't tell you because, as I just said, I am not privy to Mr. Wolfe's thought processes. But please, do not take personally what Mr. Wolfe said to you on your last trip here. He's like that with everybody."

"All right, Archie. But I will be ready for anything."

Okay, I had gotten what I felt were the easiest ones out of the way. Next was Faith Richmond, who, like the first two, I reached on my first try. She made a dismissive sound when I told her the reason for my call.

"I must say that I am puzzled, Mr. Goodwin. Just what is likely to be gained by having this meeting?"

"Your question is a good one. All I can tell you at this point is that Nero Wolfe is a genius, so he must have figured out something that he wants to share with all of us."

"Am I the first one who has been invited to this . . . whatever you call it?"

"No, Miss Richmond."

"Others have already said they would come?"

"Yes."

"Has everyone Nero Wolfe plans to invite accepted?"

"No. I have not finished my telephoning."

"Very well. If and when all the others have agreed to attend this gathering—and I mean *everyone*—then call me again, and I will consider accepting the invitation." I started to reply, but La Richmond cut me off with a curt "good-bye" before hanging up. So much for manners.

Next up: Boyd Tatum. My luck held—he too was at home. "Ah, Mr. Goodwin, somehow I felt I would be hearing from you again, and soon. What do you see as the purpose of this . . . *mass* meeting?"

"All I can tell you is that Nero Wolfe wants to discuss Arthur Wordell's death. Beyond that, I am afraid that I am in the dark myself."

"But you are his trusted assistant; surely you must know something about the program," he insisted.

"So one would be tempted to think. But Mr. Wolfe happens to keep his cards very close to his vest, to use a poker term."

After a long pause, Tatum spoke: "Well, yes . . . I guess that I can be there. Nine o'clock, you say?"

"Yes, sir."

"And who else will be present?"

"That is to be determined, but it is our intent to invite all those who had close ties to Mr. Wordell."

Tatum still sounded doubtful about the project, and I'm sure he did not believe me when I said I had no idea where Wolfe was going. On many occasions in the past, I was aware of who my boss was going to nail at one of these sessions. This time, however, I really was in the dark, to the point where I wasn't sure whether Wolfe had even figured it out himself.

I knew my luck was due to run out after reaching four people on the first try, and it did. I got no answer from my calls to Mason and Banks. Next, I dialed Nadia, who picked up her phone quickly.

"What is Mr. Wolfe going to tell all of us?" she asked when I told her about the plan for Thursday night.

"I honestly don't know," I said. "But in the past, these sessions have resulted in someone being accused of one crime or another. Mr. Wolfe has had a very good track record."

"I will ask the same question that I did before: Can my godfather come with me?"

"By all means you may bring Mr. Hewitt along," I said, knowing that Wolfe would not object.

I then continued my quest, calling Alexis Wordell, who, not surprisingly, turned out to be difficult.

"Why in the world do I need to show up for a travesty staged by that mountebank you work for?" she demanded.

"I should think that as the wife of the deceased, you would be interested in any conversation that might shed light upon how he died," I replied. And in case you are wondering, I know the meaning of *mountebank* because it had been used to describe Wolfe on previous occasions, so I had looked it up. Definitions include: *an imposter, a swindler*, and *one who deceives others to trick them out of their money*. Take your pick.

Alexis took her time responding to my comment. "What would be gained by my presence at this, this *séance*?"

"Perhaps some closure," I suggested to her. "What have you got to lose by showing up?"

"Who else will be attending?"

"People who were close to Mr. Wordell."

"One of whom might have pushed him from that window perch?"

"That certainly is a possibility."

Another long pause. "All right, I will be there, although I am not the least bit enthusiastic about this summons."

I didn't have an answer to her comment, so I simply said we would see her Thursday night.

So far, my batting average had been just about what I had expected: five and a half out of eight on the first pass—the half being Faith Richmond, who said she would grace us with her presence only if everyone else agreed to show up.

CHAPTER 25

I reported to Wolfe on my progress when he came down from the plant rooms just after eleven, and he merely nodded and rang for beer, seemingly more focused on the day's mail, which I had as usual stacked on his desk blotter.

"Aren't you interested in the reactions that I got from my calls requesting their presence?"

"Not particularly," he replied without bothering to look up as he read a letter from an orchid grower in California who was coming to New York and hoped to see Wolfe's collection.

"So it is that I toil in the wilderness," I said in a tone meant to indicate a lament. "Just out of curiosity, have you figured out who helped Arthur Wordell to end his life?" I got no response, nor did I expect one. Assuming I would be able to persuade Banks and Mason to join our gathering, it figured to be an unusual evening. Little did I know how unusual.

■ ■ ■

After lunch, Wolfe did battle with the London *Sunday Times* crossword puzzle, solving it as usual, while I ambled over to Seventh Avenue for my fortnightly haircut. My Italian barber, Charles, was still fuming about a game the Knicks had blown to the Boston Celtics the night before after having led right up until the last minute, so the two of us ended up discussing the many reasons we felt the team needed a new coach, and who that coach should be. We accomplished nothing, but at least it took my mind off our current case and my boss's refusal to communicate with me.

When I got back to the brownstone, Wolfe was up on the roof with Theodore Horstmann playing with his orchids. I have as little as possible to do with Horstmann, who thinks that any plant that is not an orchid must automatically be a weed.

Having the office to myself, I returned to my assignment, dialing Henry Banks's number. After several rings he picked up and I made my pitch.

"Thursday night? Can you tell me what's going to happen then?"

"Mr. Wolfe has not shared the details with me, but the subject, of course, will be Arthur Wordell's death."

"That sounds pretty vague to me."

"Agreed, but right now, it is all that I have got to go on. However, it is enough that almost every one of those closest to Wordell has already agreed to come to the brownstone."

"Hmm. Well, I have got a dinner engagement tomorrow night, but to be honest, it's not really all that important, and I can postpone it if you think I should."

"I would strongly advise you to be part of the gathering here."

"All right, I will show up. Any instructions?"

"No, just come prepared to hear Nero Wolfe expound as only he can."

That drew a chuckle from Banks, who seemed to have the best sense of humor of any of our suspects.

Now for the toughest nut of all, Roger Mason. Success of a sort—he was home and did not seem the least bit impressed when I identified myself. "Yes, what is it?" he mumbled.

When I told Mason about the Thursday night gathering, his mumble became a grumble. "So the great Nero Wolfe is going to identify a murderer, is that what I should expect?"

"Perhaps. On more than one occasion, that has been the result of one of these meetings."

"And who will he name tomorrow night?"

"I don't know, because he hasn't shared it with me. That's what makes my job so, well . . . interesting."

"Who else will be there?"

"Everyone whom you would expect," I told him.

That drew a "humph," from Mason, followed by a loud exhale and a reluctant, "So, at nine o'clock, you say?"

I confirmed the time, and we rang off. I wasn't done, though; I needed to get back to Faith Richmond.

"All right, now what is it this time?" came her sharp response after I had identified myself.

"You asked me to inform you when all the others who were invited to tomorrow night's gathering had accepted the invitation."

"I am frankly surprised to hear that. Tell me exactly who will be in attendance," Faith demanded. I read off the list, and she sniffed, much like she had during our earlier conversation.

"What do you think the reaction would be if I did not show up for this performance of Nero Wolfe's?"

"I can't predict for sure, although my guess is that your absence would certainly raise a few eyebrows."

"Well, that is not necessarily a bad thing, is it?" she said.

"I suppose that depends upon your point of view, Miss Richmond."

"Will anyone other than those you named be present?"

"Nadia Wordell will be bringing her godfather, Lewis Hewitt, who also, coincidentally, is a longtime friend of Nero Wolfe. Beyond that, I cannot say."

"Your boss pretty much keeps you in the dark, doesn't he? Or might you just be playing dumb?"

"Sometimes dumb comes naturally to me," I said. "Can we expect you tomorrow night?"

"Oh . . . I suppose so," Faith said. "It might prove instructive to see Nero Wolfe in action, so to speak. So far, I have been unimpressed with him."

"I hope you are not disappointed tomorrow night," I told her, and we said our good-byes. When Wolfe came down from the plant rooms at six, I was able to tell him I had corralled the whole group.

"Satisfactory," he said, ringing for beer. "Will Inspector Cramer still be in his office?"

"I would give odds on it. He comes to work late, goes home late. Do you want me to find out?"

"I do," he said, and I dialed a number that I knew by heart. Cramer answered as Wolfe picked up his instrument.

"Mr. Cramer, this is Nero Wolfe. I am having a meeting tomorrow night at my home regarding the death of Arthur Wordell, at nine o'clock. You may wish to be present."

"Don't tell me, let me guess," the inspector snarled. "You're going to throw one of your charades, right?"

"I prefer to term it a discourse."

"Whatever pleases you, by all means. Care to give me some specifics?"

"I do not, sir."

"Pardon me if I don't act surprised. I plan to bring Stebbins along."

"Pardon me if I don't act surprised," Wolfe responded, proving that he really does possess a sense of humor, however much he hides it.

CHAPTER 26

For as many times as Wolfe has gathered suspects in his office for one of his revelations—or in this case a "discourse"—I have never been able to get over my premeeting anxiety, and I simply can't explain it. Wolfe himself never seems the slightest bit on edge during the hours leading up to one of these climactic sessions. In this case, he seemed so unconcerned that when I asked if he had any preferences as to how our guests should be seated, he dismissed my question with a shrug, which would turn out to be one of his rare missteps.

I work to find ways to keep busy, while he blithely goes about his daily schedule as usual: breakfast in his bedroom; two hours up in the plant rooms in the morning and again in the afternoon; conferences with Fritz about meals and their preparation; dictating letters to me; a few chapters in one of his latest books; and of course, beer upon beer.

Typing up his letters occupied at least a portion of my day, as did my entering orchid germination records on file cards and balancing the checkbook. But after I had disposed of those chores and put a shine on two pairs of shoes, it was still only midafternoon.

So while Wolfe was upstairs puttering in his glassed-in playground with the orchids, I began arranging the office for our visitors: I put seven chairs in two rows in front of Wolfe's desk, where Wolfe could see them all without having to swivel his neck. I also placed two chairs behind the seven for Cramer and Stebbins, although they sometimes chose to stand with their backs against the wall. The red leather chair at one end of his desk was reserved for our client, Nadia Wordell, while Lewis Hewitt would be off to one side, on a sofa as an observer.

I made sure the drink cart against one wall was fully stocked with various brands of scotch, bourbon, gin, vodka, and rye, along with red, white, and rosé wines, mixers, and a silver bucket that I would later fill with ice cubes. Wolfe felt a host should be prepared for any contingency where refreshments were concerned, and I knew who would get blamed if we failed to fulfill our role with our guests.

Fritz normally got as nervous as I did on these days. He was happy that Wolfe was working, but he always worried that something might go wrong. I invariably ended up trying to soothe him in these situations, although I was hardly in a soothed condition myself.

At dinner, Wolfe chose to expound on why third-party candidates have been unsuccessful in presidential elections. My lone contribution was a piece of family lore that got passed down regarding my grandfather back home in Ohio, who voted for Theodore Roosevelt as the ill-starred "Bull Moose" party's candidate in 1912. But even that tidbit is more than I usually add to the discussion, and it got Wolfe started on the career of Teddy, whom he termed "one of our most interesting and complex presidents."

For me, the evening dragged on, and it was something of a relief when at 8:45 Inspector Cramer and Sergeant Purley Stebbins rang our doorbell. "You are the first to arrive," I told their grim faces as I let them in.

"I can't tell you that I'm happy to be here," Cramer said, while Stebbins merely sneered. Purley and I have had a mutual nonadmiration relationship that goes back years. The only question is which of us dislikes the other more.

"I see the host plans to make one of his grand entries," Cramer said as he stepped into the office and took note of the empty chair behind Wolfe's desk.

"But of course he does; did you expect anything different?" I asked.

Before Cramer could respond, the doorbell rang again and I headed down the hall. It was our client, Nadia, along with Lewis Hewitt. She clearly was nervous, while Hewitt appeared to be his usual imperturbable self. After taking their coats and hanging them up, I showed them to the office, directing Nadia to the red leather chair at the end of Wolfe's desk and motioning Hewitt to the sofa.

The doorbell squawked yet again, and I regretted that I had not asked our favorite freelance operative, Saul Panzer, to help me greet the guests and get them settled. I swung open the door and faced one smile—Zondra Zagreb—and one frown—Roger Mason. They had arrived on our stoop together, but it was clear by their body language and their expressions that they had not come together.

I ushered both in and started down the hall with them when the bell told me more guests were here. This time, it was Henry

Banks and Emory Sterling, each of whom greeted me with a smile. If they weren't happy to be part of tonight's gathering, they chose not to show it.

That left Boyd Tatum, Alexis Wordell, and Faith Richmond as the absentees. I figured Tatum would make it, but I wasn't so sure about the women. Neither of them had shown any enthusiasm whatever for the gathering, despite each saying she would be present.

But when next the bell rang, I went to the door and found myself facing Faith Richmond, who wore a black beret and a scowl. As she stepped in, I spotted Tatum stepping out of a cab and looking up at me with a grin, albeit forced.

I welcomed them both, did the coat-hanging routine, and reminded them that they knew the way to the office. I pivoted to close the front door but stopped myself. A familiar black Bentley sedan was pulling up in front of the brownstone. Alexis Evans Farrell Wordell had arrived, the last to arrive as she surely had planned.

I nodded her in and hung her sable jacket on the rack, getting a tight smile as my thank-you. When I got to the office with her, all the others had seated themselves—Emory Sterling, Henry Banks, Zondra Zagreb, and Boyd Tatum in the front row, with Tatum on the end nearest the door to the hall, and Faith Richmond and Roger Mason behind them. Having no option, Alexis sat in the remaining chair, also closest to the door in her row.

I then took drink orders. "I did not realize I was being invited to a cocktail party, or I would have worn something more appropriate," Faith Richmond said in an acid tone. "I will have a scotch."

"I know, with ice only, no water," I said. "Mr. Tatum, I believe you prefer soda with your scotch. Mr. Banks, I recall that it is rye and water, right? And Mr. Mason, is it still beer for you?"

"Very impressive," Tatum said.

"Years of practice," I responded. "Would anyone else like refreshments?"

"I believe that I will have a vodka and tonic," Sterling said, "if it is not too much trouble."

"What I would like to know," Mason said, "is what are they doing here?" He gestured with a thumb to Cramer and Stebbins.

I responded, "They are Inspector Cramer and Sergeant Stebbins of the—"

"I know who they are, obviously!" Mason snapped. "Every one of us here has probably been questioned by them. What I want to know is *why* they are here. And by the way, where is Nero Wolfe?"

"I am right here, Mr. Mason," Wolfe said as he walked into the room and settled into the reinforced chair behind his desk. "I see Mr. Goodwin is supplying a number of you with beverages, and I will be having beer."

"The presence of members of the police department strikes me as highly irregular," Faith Richmond put in.

"Does their presence make you uncomfortable?" Wolfe posed.

"I . . ." She looked around as if seeking support for her position and, finding none, said, "Oh, what difference does it really make? I feel as if we have been shanghaied here."

"No one has forced you to come, madam," Wolfe said. "You are free to leave at any time."

"Sure, and then I will probably be followed, right? I'm sure you have got more police outside just waiting for something to happen," Faith said, directing her comment at Cramer, who merely shrugged. As would later become evident, Cramer and

Stebbins had come to the brownstone without backup, which I would have reason to regret.

"Just to be clear," Wolfe addressed the assemblage once the drinks were served and everyone had more or less settled down, "I have been engaged by Nadia Wordell, who feels that her father was pushed to his death from that window ledge in Midtown."

"Now that we have settled established the identity of your client, just who is that gentleman?" Mason persisted, pointing at Hewitt over on the sofa.

"That is Lewis Hewitt, a longtime acquaintance of mine and also the godfather of Nadia Wordell. Does anyone object to his presence?" Wolfe asked, looking at each of those gathered in turn. No one spoke.

"Very well. Now I—"

"Wait a minute," Mason cut in, looking over his shoulder at Cramer. "What do the police think about Arthur's death?"

"Our investigation is ongoing," the inspector said.

"Just what is your purpose in being here?" Mason demanded.

"Mr. Cramer did not come tonight to be interrogated," Wolfe growled after draining half the beer from his glass. "I will rephrase my earlier question: Is anyone uncomfortable having him and Sergeant Stebbins present?"

Wolfe had put the man in a bind. Mason fidgeted in his chair, then spat a word I will not repeat and threw his hands up in a gesture of mock surrender. Some of the others glared at him, but no one spoke.

"Now if we may move ahead," Wolfe said, "each of the seven of you seated before me has at one time or another had what might be termed a difference of opinion with the late Mr. Wordell. And I—"

That brought a cacophony of complaints: "Just because I once argued with Arthur doesn't mean . . ." "How can you say our minor disagreements would cause me to . . ." "I take offense at the suggestion that . . ."

"Enough!" Wolfe slapped a palm down of his desk, silencing the dissonance. "If necessary, I can list examples of conflict between each of you and Mr. Wordell that might be worth discussing in detail."

"Stop right there, Mr. Wolfe," Zondra Zagreb said. "I will save you the trouble, at least in my case. The rest of you"—she looked around—"almost surely are not aware of this, but I became deeply involved with Arthur about three—" That brought a gasp from Faith Richmond and a look of shock from Nadia.

"That's right, Faith, believe it or not, he and I had an affair; there is no sense calling it anything else," Zondra said. "And Arthur was the one who broke it off, so I suppose I could easily be cast as the spurned woman who then exacted her revenge upon her lover by pushing him off a window ledge. I do have an artistic temperament, you know, which I suppose would brand me as the excitable or erratic type."

"It is utter nonsense to suspect Miss Zagreb of anything," Emory Sterling put in. "Can any of you imagine her committing murder because of what transpired between her and Arthur? Now I can't and I won't speak for any of the rest of you, but Arthur and I had our flare-ups, and I suspect each one of you had moments of discord with him as well.

"Let us face facts," Sterling continued. "He was not the easiest of men to get along with. Mr. Wolfe apparently has learned things about all of us that might—or might not—have led to a fatal confrontation."

"Okay, Emory, we all know how much you like the sound of your own mellifluous voice, but just what is the point that you are trying to make?" Faith Richmond asked in a demanding tone.

"That Mr. Wolfe could easily suspect any one of us of having at least some animosity toward Arthur," Sterling responded. "Is there anyone among us who has not exchanged harsh words with him?"

"Perhaps you are correct, but do any of the relatively petty squabbles each of us may have had with Arthur constitute grounds for, well . . . for murder?" Henry Banks asked, looking around at the others.

"Mr. Banks raises a most valid point," Wolfe said. "Based on what I have learned about each of you and your relations with Mr. Wordell, it would appear that none of your differences with him have been of sufficient import to warrant murdering the man."

"If that is the case, then just why in the hell are we all here?" Mason demanded, starting to rise. "This seems to be nothing but an exercise in futility and a waste of time for all of us!"

"Sit down!" Wolfe snapped. "We are far from done. It is my belief that Mr. Wordell's death was not the result of a premeditated act, but rather that it grew out of what Mr. Banks has termed a 'petty squabble.' "

"Go on," Cramer urged.

"Yes, sir, I will. It is my belief that the individual who was at least in part responsible for Mr. Wordell's fatal fall had come to his dreary Midtown office at night in the hopes of forcing him to—"

"Oh, oh! I'm going to be sick!" Boyd Tatum keened, holding his stomach, getting to his feet, and darting out into the hall.

"There is a powder room to the right," I yelled, but Tatum turned to the left instead, and as everyone gaped, he took his hands away from his stomach and broke into a sprint down the hall toward the front door.

CHAPTER 27

I chastise myself for what happened that night. Oh, I suppose a few others should bear their share of the responsibility, including Nero Wolfe and Inspector Cramer, but I feel that I must shoulder the brunt of the blame. That being the case, I suppose it is only fitting that because of my carelessness, my face ended up looking like it ran into a volley of strong rights from Rocky Marciano's gloved fist.

Mistake No. 1: Wolfe's neglect in suggesting a seating plan for the suspects. This permitted Tatum to occupy the chair closest to the office door, allowing for his fast exit from the brownstone.

Mistake No. 2: Cramer not ordering backup, as was usually the case when Wolfe orchestrated one of his so-called charades.

Mistake No. 3: My being far too slow in my pursuit of Tatum.

By the time I got out to the hall, Tatum had already gone out the front door and disappeared into the night. When I reached the bottom of our steps, I could see him chugging east toward Tenth Avenue. I knew that he lived down in the Village, so why would he be heading toward a *northbound* thoroughfare? I was beginning to get the picture.

Tatum surprised me with his speed, especially given his age and build. I got far enough along the block to see him hop into a cab that raced away. There were no other taxis in sight when I got to Tenth, and I ended up waiting at least a minute and maybe longer for a Yellow. I gave the hackie an address east of Broadway and north of Times Square. By now, you probably have figured out my destination.

As we pulled up in front of the drab office building, two guys in coveralls and smoking cigarettes were on the sidewalk pitching pennies.

"Have either of you seen anybody go inside in the last few minutes?" I asked as I got out of the cab and paid the driver.

"Yeah, a kinda pudgy fellow, he ran in like he was being chased, although nobody seemed to be following him," one of them answered.

"Wrong—I was the chaser, but I got outhustled," I said, handing him a dime along with a fin for his trouble. "Call the cops right now and tell them there's trouble up on the twentieth floor, plenty of trouble."

It took seemingly ages for the old elevator to come back down from where Tatum had gotten out, and the ride back up also seemed like it took forever. When I got to twenty, Tatum apparently had just gone in after having broken the pebbled glass on the door, probably with one of his shoes, which was lying on the floor and which allowed him to turn the knob from the inside.

He was headed for the window, but I figured I would catch him before he got there.

Mistake No. 4: Underestimating the strength and desire of a short, desperate middle-aged man who was determined to kill himself.

Tatum picked up one of the wooden, straight-backed chairs in that room and hurled it at me. His aim was good—too good, and I'm pretty sure I screamed as I fell after the impact. It was only later that I remembered what a Hollywood stuntman had told me several years back when Lily and I had visited a movie studio in Los Angeles, where a friend of hers worked in set design.

"The chairs that we hit each other over the head with in those bar fights are made of balsa or something lightweight like that, or we'd all be bloody before the end of the scene," the stuntman said. "The audio boys make it sound like we're really getting whacked, when actually those so-called chairs fall apart almost silently on impact. But keep that to yourself, okay? Remember that we're making magic out here, and we don't want the folks back home in Keokuk to see behind the curtain."

It turned out that I was all bloody myself as I crawled across the floor toward Tatum, every move causing a stabbing pain in my face. Whatever strength he had in running and then throwing that chair at me had deserted Tatum as he tried to pull up the window. He was still straining to lift it when I got to my knees with effort and grabbed him around the legs, dragging him down to the floor. He started pounding me on the head with his fists, and I held on until someone pulled me off.

"It's okay, we got him now, Goodwin," came a familiar voice. I wiped the blood from my eyes and looked into the face of Purley Stebbins. Never had that big, square mug of his looked so good.

Stebbins wasn't alone in the room. There also were two uniformed cops, probably called by the men I had met downstairs.

I have a vague memory of Cramer walking in and barking orders before I totally conked out.

CHAPTER 28

I ended up in the hospital overnight, having gotten a couple of stitches over my right eye and another three on my chin. Tatum's aim had been dead-on. At least my nose had been more or less spared, or it would have become even flatter than it already is.

Wolfe didn't visit me, but he did send an arrangement of yellow and rose *Odontoglossum*s that the nurses all fawned over. When I checked out, I gave them to my favorite, a curvy redhead who was good at fluffing my pillows and holding my hand with her own soft paws when she checked my pulse.

Lily later chided me for not telling her I was in the hospital. "I would have come and smuggled scotch to you in a flask, Escamillo," she said, "sort of like a latter-day Florence Nightingale or Clara Barton. Or maybe somebody out of a Hemingway novel. I really do hope that you were not a difficult patient."

I still had bandages on my face when I returned home, having been picked up in the Heron sedan by Saul Panzer on

Wolfe's orders. "Lovin' babe, you look like you got smacked by a freight train," Saul said, shaking his head. "And to think, you missed a poker game for *that*."

I agreed with Saul that life wasn't fair. At home, Wolfe was as close as he ever gets to being solicitous, asking about the degree of my pain and whether I would prefer that Fritz serve me lunch and dinner up in my room.

"I am okay eating in the dining room as long as my presence does not detract from your appetite," I told him. He assured me that he would bear up despite my mangled appearance.

On my second day back, I was in the office typing up correspondence from Wolfe to an orchid grower in Louisiana when he came down from the plant room at a minute or two past eleven. The doorbell rang, and I ambled down the hall, noting a familiar figure in the one-way glass.

"Inspector Cramer has come calling upon us," I told Wolfe as I returned to the office.

"Let him in," he said with a sigh, and I followed orders.

"You've looked better," the inspector observed as he went down the hall to the office.

"Thanks a whole heap," I responded as he settled into the red leather chair and pulled out a cigar, which as usual he did not light.

"To what do we owe the honor of this visit?" Wolfe inquired, his expression impassive.

"Getting pretty formal now, aren't we?" Cramer said, gnawing on the stogie.

"Please enlighten us," Wolfe replied.

"As I guess that you—or at least Goodwin—figured out, Tatum was actually going to kill himself the same way Wordell had died. He told one of my men after Goodwin stopped him that 'It's only fair I end it this way. Just let me jump!' "

"The moment he darted out of the office, I knew exactly where he was heading," Wolfe said.

"Uh-huh, so you say. Anyway, Tatum was a blubbering mess when we started questioning him," Cramer said. "He told us that he had gone that night to see Wordell and make one more try at getting him to agree to a biography. He said he already had a publisher lined up who had promised him an advance.

"Tatum said that when he got to the dump of an office, Wordell was sitting on that sill of his looking out over whatever it was that fascinated him. Here's what he told us," Cramer said, pulling a folded sheet from his breast pocket.

I went right up to Arthur and told him about the offer I had gotten from a publisher. His response was to laugh in my face and tell me that he did not give a good goddamn whether I had a publisher or not, that he wasn't interested. He reminded me of the letter he sent me saying the same things. Then he told me to get the hell out of there, that he was meditating.

I laughed at that, and Arthur sneered and shook his fist at me. I leaned out and grabbed at his fist in anger, and he lost his balance trying to take a swing at me. Then I think that I gave him a shove, just a light shove, hardly more than a nudge, and . . . well, just like that he was gone; he didn't even make a sound. I just left the building then. Nobody saw me.

"How will Mr. Tatum be charged?" Wolfe asked.

"Probably with murder, at least that's what we have been hearing from the D.A.'s office, although Tatum's lawyers probably will try for manslaughter or accidental death," Cramer said. "However, the fact that he tried to kill himself the same way Wordell died is pretty damning evidence against him. Then there's the issue of assault and battery against Goodwin, if he chooses to press the issue."

"That is solely Archie's decision," Wolfe said.

"Ah, I will pass on that," I said, waving it away with a hand. "If he covers any medical costs my insurance doesn't, that's good enough for me."

"Well, you sure threw me off by referring to the evening as a 'discourse,'" Cramer said to Wolfe. "I didn't think you were going to name a suspect. If I had, there would have been backup outside of your place. We would have grabbed Tatum, and Goodwin wouldn't look like he had been run over by a steamroller."

"Thanks so much for your kind thoughts," I said with the sourest tone I could muster.

"I must also shoulder a portion of the blame," Wolfe said. "I did not object when Mr. Tatum took a seat closest to the door."

"Did you suspect him all along?" Cramer asked.

Wolfe paused before answering, which I found interesting. "I was . . . suspicious. He had told us he had visited Mr. Wordell in his Midtown office only once, yet Wordell's secretary, a Miss Courtney, told Archie that he had been there on several occasions."

"That's pretty thin, not a lot to go on," Cramer observed.

"No, sir, it is not, although it should have been enough. But I am sure you have had cases yourself where the clues were well hidden and easy to overlook. I am being a poor host, drinking beer in your presence. Can we offer you something to drink?"

"In the morning? Oh, hell, why not. I'll have one of those beers like you've got, just to take away the coffee taste in my mouth."

Later that day, as Wolfe was having his afternoon session with the orchids, I got a call from Nadia Wordell.

"How are you feeling, Archie? I understand you got hurt that night after you rushed out chasing after Mr. Tatum."

"Yes, it's fair to say that I did get a little banged up, but I am happy to report that I seem to be recovering, although not as fast as I would like. Things must have gotten very interesting in the brownstone after Tatum and I both tore out of there in one hell of a hurry."

"Yes, it was strange, to say the least. Nobody knew quite what to do, even including your Mr. Wolfe. For several seconds, it was very quiet, and then Mr. Wolfe said something about the Midtown building where Daddy had that office, and Inspector Cramer and his sergeant darted out every bit as fast as you had.

"Finally, we all began leaving one at a time, unsure of what to make of what happened. It wasn't until later that I learned from my godfather that you had been hurt. I'm glad to hear you're on the mend. I was hoping to come by at a time convenient for you and Mr. Wolfe and write a check."

"I will talk to him and let you know. How are you doing after all that has happened?"

"Oh, all right, I guess. I was surprised to learn that Mr. Tatum was . . . well, was the one. I never would have suspected him."

"That is so often the case," I told her. "You will be hearing from me, soon, I'm sure."

Wolfe had suggested that Nadia come to the brownstone at eleven the next day, and she was prompt, giving me another of her shy smiles as I seated her in the red leather chair. Wolfe came in a minute later, dipped his chin in a greeting to our guest, sat, and pushed the button to call for beer.

"Are you satisfied with the outcome of this undertaking?" he asked, leaning back and placing his hands palms down on the desk.

She lifted her shoulders and let them drop. "As I have already told Archie, I certainly did not expect Boyd Tatum to be my father's killer, although I guess *killer* might be a strong word, given that he says he really didn't mean for things to end up the way they did. But you were able to figure things out, and for that I am more grateful than I can say," she said, pulling out a checkbook. "We have never talked about a figure before, but I know from my godfather that you are expensive—and worth it. Would fifty thousand dollars be fair?"

"More than fair," Wolfe said, holding up a palm as if to suggest that it was too much.

"I have never been good as a negotiator," she replied. "I believe that figure is an amount that you have earned." Nero Wolfe has never been one to turn down money pressed upon him, and this was not to be an exception.

I saw Nadia to the door, and she held out a hand, which I took in mine. "Archie, I don't suppose that we will ever meet again," she told me. "You are every bit as nice as Lily has described you. Thank you so much for everything that you have done."

I watched her walk down the steps to the street, silently wishing her a happy life. I believe she merited it.

CHAPTER 29

As Nadia had predicted, our paths haven't crossed again and probably will not, although Lewis Hewitt has kept us apprised of his goddaughter's activities. For one, she decided not to give her father's art collection to the new Guggenheim. She took the advice of Emory Sterling and sent portions of the collection to museums specializing in specific genres and periods.

Trying to put the past in a rearview mirror, Nadia has moved to Paris, where, so Lily tells me, she has an apartment on the Left Bank and is taking courses at the Sorbonne, something she had always dreamed of doing. Lily also says Nadia has found herself a love interest, a young Parisian artist who wants to move to somewhere in the south of France. Lily, who corresponds with Nadia, has the suspicion that she may eventually settle there with him.

Nadia also made peace of a sort with her father's widow. Alexis waived all rights (if indeed she had any) to the Wordell art collection, and in return, Nadia sold Alexis her father's brownstone in Yorkville at the price that she, Nadia, asked, according to Hewitt. It seems that Alexis had always coveted the residence, and now it was hers in which to throw parties and host salons.

In October, the Guggenheim opened to great fanfare as well as slings of criticism. Its architect, Frank Lloyd Wright, did not live to see the building's completion, having died six months earlier. Lily went to one of the opening galas and said it was among the social events of the year, although she like many others was less than enthused about the museum's radical design. I turned down the opportunity to be her escort, ceding my position to Lewis Hewitt, who is far more comfortable at events like this.

Zondra Zagreb has continued to make a name for herself in the world of abstract expressionism, and Lily even got me to attend another one of her openings at a gallery on Madison Avenue. Her work never has made it into the Guggenheim as she had hoped, although she recently landed a good review in the *Gazette*, whose art critic called her work "exciting and dynamic."

Faith Richmond has continued to write biographies of artists, and one of her recent works, about an American "outsider" artist, was reviewed in the *Times* book section, where her prose was described as "incisive" and "perceptive."

Roger Mason, his reputation battered by his experience with Arthur Wordell, has returned to the relative safety of New England, where he has been named the director of a museum in the Boston area.

Emory Sterling continues in his role as editor and publisher of *Art & Artists* magazine, where he got in a last word of sorts. His publication recently ran a lengthy "in memoriam" article about Arthur Wordell and his collection, which included an extensive portfolio of color reproductions of his art. How Wordell would have bristled at that.

Henry Banks has relocated to Southern California, where he has been selected to curate the collection of a multimillionaire industrialist who has dreams of eventually opening a museum displaying his collection in Los Angeles.

Boyd Tatum's court case continues to drag on. His lawyers have argued that he should be charged with manslaughter, although the state is pushing for a tougher murder charge, arguing as Inspector Cramer had earlier that Tatum's attempted suicide was in effect an admission of guilt. Lon Cohen says the *Gazette*'s legal affairs columnist thinks the whole business could last for months, or maybe years, with each side pushing for continuances.

As for Nero Wolfe, I have never been totally convinced that he knew Boyd Tatum was the guilty party. I felt that as he was talking to the assemblage, he was stalling for time, perhaps hoping someone would implicate himself, which is what of course happened, although not in the way that he—or I—had expected.

Lily Rowan is treating me to dinner tonight at Rusterman's, the one restaurant that Wolfe will deign to eat at himself on those extremely rare occurrences when he leaves the brownstone to dine. Normally when Lily and I go out, I foot the bill, but this is an exception—a celebration of the last bandage having been removed from my face. There is not a lot of bruising left from the impact of that chair, and Lily says I look almost normal again, which I will take as a compliment—I think.

After a superb dinner, we strolled in the gentle evening air and found ourselves on Park Avenue passing the Waldorf Astoria. "Say, how about an after-dinner drink in that very watering hole where we first discussed Arthur Wardell and that cast of characters at the Guggenheim dinner?" I asked.

"That sounds good to me, Escamillo, but on one condition," Lily replied, "which is that I buy. Remember, this whole evening is my treat."

"I grudgingly accept," I told her, trying without success to sound grudging.

We settled into the very booth we had occupied on that not-so-long-ago evening and found ourselves being served by the same waiter as before. After we had gotten our drinks, I winked at Lily. "So, at any point along the way, did you think Tatum was the one who dispatched the famed collector?"

"You do have a way of putting a girl on the spot, don't you?" she replied, arching an eyebrow. "If you must know, I always suspected Henry Banks, although I'm not sure that I can tell you why. He just always seemed somewhat unctuous to me. That means oily, or smug."

"I do happen to know what it means," I said with a grin.

"Oh, of course you do," Lily said. "Having been around Nero Wolfe for so long, you probably have become a walking dictionary. Anyway, Banks was my choice. I never would have picked Boyd Tatum. But then, I've never claimed to be a detective."

"I certainly wouldn't have chosen him either," I said. "And I'm not entirely sure Wolfe did, either."

That drew a healthy laugh from Lily. "It just goes to show that nobody's perfect, Escamillo. And now," she said, raising her glass, "here's a toast to your full recovery from getting a chair in the face."

Now there was something I could drink to with enthusiasm.

I read in the *Gazette* a few days later that a half-empty twenty-three-story Midtown building was slated for demolition to make way for a glass-and-steel office tower more than twice its height, with its principal tenant an oil company.

I started to turn the page when I realized that I had knowledge of the old building—too much knowledge, and I proceeded to read the rest of the article. A spokesman for the building's owners was quoted as saying that the structure had outlived its usefulness. When the *Gazette* reporter asked whether Arthur Wordell's fatal plunge had anything to do with razing the building, his reply: "No comment."

I briefly contemplated one last visit to the spot where I punched out the moose and took a chair to the face. But I decided to let the old place get bulldozed without my being present. It was enough for me to know it would be gone and not mourned.

AUTHOR NOTES

This story is set in the late 1950s, and its characters, events, and institutions are fictional with the following exceptions:

The Solomon R. Guggenheim Museum, located at Fifth Avenue and Eighty-Ninth Street, in Manhattan, was completed in 1959 and has been added onto in the ensuing years.

Frank Lloyd Wright (1867–1959), generally considered to be the most famous American architect, designed the Guggenheim Museum, the only building he created in New York City. The museum's revolutionary design, including its spiral ramp in the galleries, has been both lauded and derided in the decades since its opening. As Archie mentioned in the narrative, Wright never got to see the museum in use, dying in Arizona six months before its doors opened and shortly before his ninety-second birthday.

Louis Sullivan (1856–1924), who was mentioned by Nero Wolfe when he was talking to Frank Lloyd Wright, was a preeminent and pioneering American architect in the late-nineteenth and early-twentieth centuries and was an early employer of the young Wright.

Anne Baxter (1923–1985), Wright's granddaughter, was a Hollywood actress who won an Oscar for her role as Sophie in *The Razor's Edge*, a 1946 filmed adaptation of W. Somerset Maugham's novel. She also was nominated for an Oscar for the title role in the 1950 film *All About Eve*. And she had a starring role in Cecil B. DeMille's *The Ten Commandments* (1956), which is referenced in the narrative. She is buried in the family plot on Frank Lloyd Wright's estate in Spring Green, Wisconsin.

Rocky Marciano (1923–1969), who Archie referred to after his face had been battered, was heavyweight boxing champion from 1952 to 1956, when he retired undefeated. In his career, he won all fifty-nine of his bouts. He died in 1969, one day short of his forty-fifth birthday.

Jackson Pollock (1912–1956), who is mentioned in the story, was an American painter and a major figure in the abstract expressionist movement and was known for his style of "drip painting." He died in an automobile accident at the age of forty-four.

Bernard Baruch (1870–1965), whose autobiography Nero Wolfe was reading, was an American financier, statesman, philanthropist, and political adviser. He counseled Presidents Woodrow Wilson during World War I and Franklin D. Roosevelt during World War II.

The following newspapers referred to—the *Times*, *Daily News*, *World-Telegram*, *Herald Tribune*, *Journal American*, *Post*, and *Mirror*—all were published in New York at the time of the story. The two fictional papers in the story are the *Gazette*, which has played a role in many Nero Wolfe tales over the years, and the tabloid scandal sheet *Mail & Express*, with its Keyhole Peeper column.

As with my previous books, I have relied on several sources, including these four: *Nero Wolfe of West Thirty-Fifth Street: The Life and Times of America's Largest Private Detective* by William Baring-Gould (The Viking Press, New York, 1968); *The Nero Wolfe Cookbook* by Rex Stout and the Editors of Viking Press (Viking Press, New York, 1973); *The Brownstone House of Nero Wolfe* by Ken Darby, as told by Archie Goodwin (Little, Brown & Co., Boston, Toronto, 1983); and *Rex Stout: A Biography* by John McAleer (Little Brown & Co., Boston, 1977). The McAleer book justly won an Edgar Award in the biography category from the Mystery Writers of America.

I send my heartfelt thanks and highest regards to Rex Stout's daughter, Rebecca Stout Bradbury. She has been a source of consistent support and encouragement of my continuation of the characters and settings created so wonderfully by her father over four decades.

My thanks and appreciation also go to my agent, Martha Kaplan, to Otto Penzler and Rob Hart of Mysterious Press, and to the efficient and energetic team at Open Road Integrated Media.

And I save my warmest thanks for my wife, Janet, who has been by my side for well over fifty years, supplying enthusiastic support and—more important—unconditional love.

ABOUT THE AUTHOR

Robert Goldsborough is an American author best known for continuing Rex Stout's famous Nero Wolfe series. Born in Chicago, he attended Northwestern University and upon graduation went to work for the Associated Press, beginning a lifelong career in journalism that would include long periods at the *Chicago Tribune* and *Advertising Age*.

While at the *Tribune*, Goldsborough began writing mysteries in the voice of Rex Stout, the creator of iconic sleuths Nero Wolfe and Archie Goodwin. Goldsborough's first novel starring Wolfe, *Murder in E Minor* (1986), was met with acclaim from both critics and devoted fans, winning a Nero Award from the Wolfe Pack. Ten more Wolfe mysteries followed, including

ABOUT THE AUTHOR

Death on Deadline (1987) and *Fade to Black* (1990). In 2005, Goldsborough published *Three Strikes You're Dead*, the first in an original series starring Chicago Tribune reporter Snap Malek. *The Battered Badge* (2018) is his most recent novel.

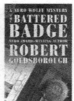

MYSTERIOUSPRESS.COM

THE MYSTERIOUS BOOKSHOP, founded in 1979, is located in Manhattan's Tribeca neighborhood. It is the oldest and largest mystery-specialty bookstore in America.

The shop stocks the finest selection of new mystery hardcovers, paperbacks, and periodicals. It also features a superb collection of signed modern first editions, rare and collectable works, and Sherlock Holmes titles. The bookshop issues a free monthly newsletter highlighting its book clubs, new releases, events, and recently acquired books.

58 Warren Street
info@mysteriousbookshop.com
(212) 587-1011
Monday through Saturday
11:00 a.m. to 7:00 p.m.

FIND OUT MORE AT:

www.mysteriousbookshop.com

FOLLOW US:

@TheMysterious and Facebook.com/MysteriousBookshop

OPEN ROAD

INTEGRATED MEDIA

Find a full list of our authors and
titles at www.openroadmedia.com

FOLLOW US
@OpenRoadMedia